AN AVALON CAREER ROMANCE

A NEW UNDERSTANDING
Debby Mayne

Patty O'Neill isn't your ordinary, run-of-the-mill auto mechanic. She's a beautiful, feminine, athletic woman who is highly skilled and specializes in repairing the engines of vintage automobiles. When Dr. Max Dillard comes to Clearview to run in the annual marathon race, he's the one who catches Patty in a fall that's the result of her lack of physical conditioning for the event. Business has been so good that she hasn't had time to train for the race.

Patty fights very hard to keep her distance from the first man she's ever thought she could fall in love with. If he didn't live so far away, it might be different, but she knows that the distance would provide more barriers than any relationship can survive. Can she resist the doctor's subtle charms?

A NEW UNDERSTANDING

•

Debby Mayne

AVALON BOOKS
NEW YORK

PRINTED IN THE UNITED STATES OF AMERICA
ON ACID-FREE PAPER
BY HADDON CRAFTSMEN, BLOOMSBURG, PENNSYLVANIA

This book is dedicated to my husband, Wally, and
daughters, Alison and Lauren,
for their love and support through the many ups and downs
of life.

Acknowledgments

Thanks to Kathy Carmichael, Kim Llewellyn, and Tara Spicer
for their encouragement and friendship.

I'm also thankful to the Tampa Area Romance Authors for the
fabulous workshops where I've learned a tremendous amount
about the craft of writing.

And thanks to editors Erin Cartwright and Mira Son
for doing such a great job with my books.

Chapter One

"Patty, we need to start looking around for some decent furniture for the waiting area," Amy said as she pulled out her brand-new leather chair from behind her desk. "If we're gonna be different, we might as well go all the way."

With a grin, Patty O'Neill nodded. She was glad she'd taken Amy up on her offer to form a partnership. What Patty lacked in finesse, Amy had in abundance.

The vast differences between their backgrounds was obvious, but Patty didn't think it mattered in their friendship. In fact, those differences enhanced it, in her opinion. They had already learned quite a bit from each other. With luck, this would continue. Patty loved new experiences.

1

"If anyone calls, I'll be in the back," Patty called over her shoulder.

"I thought you weren't working on engines today."

"I'm not, I just want to take a look at the Chevy your brother found."

With a chuckle, Amy shook her head. "Can't stay away from cars, can you, Patty?"

"It's hard," Patty replied sheepishly.

"You have to get ready for the Clearview Cross Country Run this weekend."

In one sweeping move, Patty closed the door and stepped back inside the office. "You're right. I need to go work out. I haven't done a race in so long, my muscles won't know what hit them."

"I'll have this office in tip-top shape when you get back, so don't worry about anything here."

Patty couldn't believe how easy Amy was to work with. "I hope I don't blow this race."

"You won't," Amy told her. "Just remember to pace yourself."

"Yeah, yeah. I know." Patty knew she didn't stand much of a chance to win the race, but she wanted a respectable time.

Amy seemed to understand her need for silence, which was good. Patty was afraid she might bite Amy's head off if she said too much. She was on edge.

As soon as Patty gathered up her purse and jacket, she was out the door. There were so many things she needed to do to get ready, she wasn't quite sure where to start.

On her way home she thought about the shop she and Amy had opened six months ago. Before that, they'd done six months of planning for both Amy's wedding to Zach and the grand opening of their antique car restoration business. While there were some pretty frantic moments, everything had come off without a major hitch, something she attributed to Amy's organization. Patty knew it certainly wasn't hers.

Classic Cars was a success from the instant they'd opened their doors, thanks to Zach. He'd sent so much business their way, Patty found herself working on engines from sunup to sundown six days a week. Amy had turned out to be a genius in restoring the few auto interiors they'd agreed to do. She'd studied under the best in the business and had taken her job seriously, gathering books from every major auto company and making sure the cars were brought back to their original condition. That was one less worry for Patty.

Patty's first stop on her way home was at the sports store. She needed to get her shoes for the marathon race she'd participated in every year since she'd started running.

Next, she had to deposit the day's checks for the business. It amazed her that they'd already started making enough money to start earning a salary. Thanks to Amy's trust fund and the sale of one of her best cars, they'd been able to go into business not owing anyone a dime. It was a liberating feeling. Patty knew one of the reasons most businesses failed was their lack of capital to keep the bills paid for the first couple of years. That wouldn't be a problem with Classic Cars.

When Patty got home, she headed inside and kicked off her shoes at the door. After they'd made friends, Amy had come over and worked with her to get her house fixed up.

"It has so much potential," Amy had told her. "All it needs is a little paint and some polishing, and it'll be absolutely charming."

From the looks of what they'd done, Patty knew Amy had the magic touch. She loved her place, now that it was color-coordinated with peaches, corals, and varying shades of green. Her kitchen was blue, her favorite color since she could remember. Patty's brothers and father had taught her everything they knew about cars, but interior decorating wasn't part of it.

Once they got the inside of the house looking good, Amy had surprised her with an old-fashioned paint party. A team of Amy's good friends had shown up in work clothes with paint brushes in hand. Since the house was white already, it only took one coat to make it good as new. Then, Amy and Denise brought flats of flowers to give her that extra "zing" that made the place look like it came out of a magazine. Even Patty's brothers had been impressed.

As much of a tomboy as Patty had always been, she

knew there was some femininity lurking inside her, too. She just needed someone to help her find it. So once she got out of the home she'd grown up in, she'd gone to a department store for a makeover. People she'd known all her life hadn't recognized her until she'd opened her mouth.

Patty felt wonderful about her new business, her home, and most of the things she'd managed to accomplish. But she knew one thing was missing. She'd never met a man she could even consider spending the rest of her life with.

Men seemed to either be intimidated by her or considered her one of the guys. The guys from Clearview kept reminding her of the times she'd pounded them on the playground. And men from Plattsville seemed to want to talk only about cars because that was how they'd met—at car shows. Although Patty loved cars, she wanted something else. She wanted balance. But she wasn't sure achieving it was possible.

Patty had just put a frozen dinner into the microwave when the phone rang. It was Linda, her friend who'd volunteered to coordinate the race this year.

"We have more people signed up from out of town this year than ever before," Linda told her. "I just hope everything goes off smoothly."

"I'm sure it will, with you at the helm," Patty said. Linda was very efficient, the type who didn't ever leave a stone unturned.

"Are you ready?" Linda asked.

"Yeah, as ready as I'll ever be."

"I was worried that with you starting your new business, you haven't had much time to work out."

"That's true," Patty said slowly, "but wild horses couldn't keep me from running in this race. It's one of the things I look forward to all year."

"Me, too," Linda said. "This will be the first year I haven't run in it."

"Why aren't you running?"

"There's too much other stuff to do. I don't want to be out there on the road and have something go wrong. Who'll take care of it if I'm not there?"

Patty laughed. "I understand, Linda. You're way too responsible for your own good."

"Are you calling me a control freak?"

"Well . . ."

"Can't help it," Linda said. "It's something I'm cursed with."

"Look, if you want me to teach you how to hang loose and just let things happen, let me know. I'm the champion at letting things slide."

"Uh, I don't think so, Patty," Linda said. "Look at you. Business woman extraordinaire, one of the prettiest houses in town, and a marathon runner. That's not exactly letting things slide."

"I had help."

The microwave buzzer went off, so Patty tucked the phone between her shoulder and ear, grabbed a potholder and pulled the cardboard tray out, carefully raising the plastic top to let some steam out. She took a step away from the counter and cleared a place on the table.

"I'll let you go, but I need to ask a favor," Linda told her.

"Sure, anything."

"Connie is supposed to man the sign-up booth, but she can't get here when it opens. She said she'd be a half hour late."

"Want me to sign people up?" Patty asked.

"If you don't mind."

"Of course, I don't mind." It wouldn't hurt to size up the competition.

As soon as she was off the phone, Patty set the table while her dinner cooled. Her mind raced as she ate her meal. The weather forecast for the weekend was perfect for the race, which was an enormous relief for Patty. She'd run in rain or wind, but that could make for a pretty miserable race.

It would do her good to sign people up. She was always a little nervous before she ran, and this would take the edge off. Maybe she'd stick around after Connie got there and help out a little longer.

When Patty asked Amy if she was thinking about running, Amy laughed. "I can barely walk without tripping over my own feet. But I'll be there to watch you cross the finish line."

"Stumble across the finish line, you mean?"

Patty had no doubt Amy would be right there,

Debby Mayne

cheering her on until she'd completed the race. Amy was a good friend to a fault.

After Patty finished her dinner, she stuck the utensils in the dishwasher and discarded the cardboard container. Then she went to her bedroom to try on her running clothes. It had been so long since she'd worn any of them, she wasn't sure if they would still fit. Bulges had a way of showing up in least expected places when an athlete neglected to stay in shape.

She pulled the shorts on and was relieved to see that they fit. Vowing to stay in shape this time, Patty grabbed her shirt, shoes, and socks and tried them all on.

As she stood in front of her full-length mirror, Patty's mind raced back to the last time she'd run in a race of this magnitude. She'd come in a close second, which really bugged the heck out of her. Before that, she'd won the women's division in most of her races. Now, she'd be happy with the second place win, but it was only because she knew some of those runners had been working out every day for the past several months, getting in shape, while she'd been up to her elbows in car grease.

Satisfied with the fact that she didn't have to go out and buy new clothes for the race, Patty got ready for bed.

Max had never even been to Clearview before, but he'd signed up for their annual marathon race at the suggestion of his receptionist. "It's the best in the region," she'd told him. "And it'll get you in shape for the one in Atlanta."

Every month he ran in a different race, hoping to do a little better than the time before. And he had. Now, he was up to coming in the top five in most small races and placing in the top ten percent of the larger ones. Now, if he could only win.

Winning was something that had always come naturally for Max. He'd been the smartest kid in all his classes growing up, enabling him to skip a couple of grades in elementary school. He'd earned his bachelor's degree when most of his friends were still applying to college. When Max was twenty-one, he'd become the youngest MD in the history of the state.

Now, he was the most popular of all the doctors in the Dillard Medical Group, started by his grandfather fifty years ago. No one could ever say any of his accomplishments had been given to him; even though he'd joined the family practice, Max had earned his position every step of the way, putting in late nights and long hours. He'd taken additional classes until he was able to treat almost anything his wealthy, big-city patients could conceivably come down with. Everyone loved his charm and light-hearted humor, something he'd developed as a child prodigy. However, when he got home each night, alone in his condo, the smiles faded and he was lonely.

He knew there was more to life than being a physician to pampered patients. He wanted hobbies, he wanted outside interests, he wanted friends. The problem with the last desire was that Max never knew if people liked him only because of his status as one of the most successful doctors in the large, prestigious family practice. Everyone who knew him now was familiar with his past, but new friends were hard to judge.

"I'll be out of town for a couple of weeks, Mary," Max told his medical assistant. "After the race, I thought I might do a little traveling."

Mary smiled back at him. "Have fun, Doc. You deserve it after that last ordeal with Mrs. Heston. I thought she'd never stop complaining."

"I don't know how much I deserve it, but I sure do need it." Max left the shiny chrome office rubbing the back of his neck.

All his life he'd been so busy that he hadn't had time to step back and take a good look at things. He'd been running on the fast track. What he'd always thought of as success—a successful medical practice, a nice car, and wise investments—hadn't made him happy. In fact, he found himself pretty miserable at times.

He needed to find a diversion, something to clear the cobwebs between his ears. Max knew he'd reached a point in his life when he needed to figure out a few things. Was he where he should be, in terms of personal growth and satisfaction? Obviously not, with as many doubts creeping through his mind as he'd had lately.

After the race, he planned to take a leisurely drive through the countryside in his vintage Cadillac, one of the few things he'd bought for himself. Stan, his cousin who'd just graduated from medical school and had now joined the practice, had shown him some pictures of the car, drooling over them, saying that he hoped to one day be able to buy a car like that.

Max thought about the car and got the number of the car owner from Stan. He found himself behind the wheel of it that night. One quick call to his cousin from his cell phone told him that it would be okay for him to go ahead and buy it for himself. Max didn't want to upset Stan by snagging the car out from under him, but the young man assured him he considered it an honor to be the one who'd shown him the pictures.

"You sure?" Max asked.

"Positive," Stan replied firmly. "There are other cars out there, and by the time I can afford one like that, there'll be more."

Max went straight home and grabbed the bags he'd packed and left by the door. There weren't many; he traveled light. It only took two trips before he was ready to go—one to get his things and the other to make sure lights were out and everything was locked. Since he'd be gone for a while, he didn't want to come home to a disaster.

As he drove away from his house, Max thought

about the time ahead of him. It had been so long since he'd done something like this—something that wasn't related to his practice—that he wasn't sure if he could handle it for a full two weeks. But he was darn sure gonna try. Maybe he'd come back appreciating some of the things he'd begun to dread.

The small town of Clearview was only a few hours away. Max chose country roads rather than the interstate. He wanted to get completely off the fast track and take in some of the scenery along the way.

He stopped at a quaint country store that had a small restaurant attached. This was exactly what he needed right now: home cooking.

The warmth that flooded him as he ate confirmed that he needed to slow down. This was living. What he'd been doing lately was existing. There was a big difference between the two.

By the time Max got back in his car and got a few more miles down the road, he began to relax. Now *this* was nice, he thought, as he inhaled the fresh country air that came in through the open windows of his car.

Eventually, Max noticed that several businesses had begun popping up on the side of the road, at first hundreds of yards apart, then closer. When he reached the sign that said "Welcome to Clearview," most of the stores and offices were in strip centers, which was a dead giveaway of how much the town had grown. In fact, from the looks of things, Clearview was bursting at the seams. No wonder, though. It was a beautiful town. So homey, so peaceful. Although he couldn't imagine himself actually living in a place like this, he knew it was what he needed for now.

He pulled off to the side of the road and opened his glove compartment to get the map he'd stuck in there yesterday.

Once he knew where he was in relation to his hotel, Max headed toward town. Maybe this place would give him what he needed. Or perhaps he'd have to wait until he finished this race and get his rest elsewhere. It didn't matter. He had a full two weeks to reconnect with himself.

The woman at the hotel desk was extremely pleasant. "Hi, Dr. Dillard," she said when he told her his name. "I hope you like your stay in Clearview. The weather is supposed to cooperate with us for the Clearview Cross Country Run."

"That's good," he said, backing away.

"Good luck."

He nodded as he grabbed his bag. "Thanks, Miss."

Max had never seen a hotel room quite like this one. It wasn't sleek and professionally decorated like the rooms he stayed in at medical conventions. No, this one appeared to have been decorated by someone he thought might be named Aunt Bea. The bedspread was a quilted hodge-podge of colors, the walls were painted a soft shade of ivory, and the draperies were a deep forest green with a small print pattern of diamonds in tan and burgundy. All the furniture looked like it might have come from someone's country home. There was even a picture of a duck hanging on the wall behind the bed.

That night Max slept like a log. His hotel was in the heart of downtown Clearview, so he was prepared for sounds of traffic: horns blaring, tires and brakes squealing, people yelling. However, everything was quiet. Apparently, this town rolled up and went to sleep when the sun went down.

He'd been told he could sign up early for the race, then go back to his room to get ready. This was certainly unusual, but he thought it sounded like a good idea. He'd already made reservations, and they'd taken his credit card number over the phone. All he had to do was report in.

The woman sitting at the booth was obviously either one of the runners or was dressed in athletic clothes to get in the spirit of the race. But as his gaze raked over her from head to foot, he thought she looked every bit the runner. She was very fit. And very pretty.

She turned and looked him directly in the eye. A smile quickly lit her face, which gave him a jolt of something in his abdomen. That ray of sunshine darting from her eyes was aimed directly at him. It felt good.

"Hi, there," she said as he got closer to the table. "You signed up for the race?"

Nodding, Max replied, "Yes, I'm Max Dillard. I called last month."

Her forehead crinkled as she scanned the pages in front of her. "Uh, I don't see your name here. Let me check something."

Max stood at the edge of her table, while she used her cell phone to call someone. He only heard her side of the conversation, but it didn't sound like good news.

After she clicked off, she hesitated, then turned to him. "Uh, Mr. Dillard, I'm sorry, but we don't have you down on the list. Are you sure this was the race you registered for?"

Max felt his insides churn. "I'm absolutely positive. I even gave the woman my credit card number."

If she didn't look so forlorn, Max would have been fighting mad. He had no doubt he'd signed up for this race, and by darn, he was gonna run in it. But she looked so sincere, he couldn't work up a good round of anger. He stood and glared at her as she scanned the pages once more.

Finally, after she shifted her feet for the hundredth time, she handed him the papers and said, "Why don't you look over these names and see if we might have made a mistake?" She stood up. "I'm gonna try to call someone else who might have another list."

Max paused for a moment, then nodded and took the papers with a forced smile. This was a first for him, but at least she was trying to solve the problem.

He half-heartedly scanned the list as he watched the woman out of the corner of his eye. She spoke into her cell phone about twenty feet away. He couldn't hear what she was saying, but he knew she was trying to help him.

When she got off the phone, she came back to the table. "See anything that looks like it might be you?"

"No, and I'm not likely to, either. Someone has made a big mistake."

"Yeah," she said, "it happens. But I've never heard of Linda messing up like this in all the years I've run this race."

"Linda," Max said, snapping his fingers. "That's the name of the woman I spoke to. Is she around here somewhere?"

"No, not yet," the woman said. "She'll be here later."

"Look, Miss," Max said, "I just want to sign in and go back to my hotel. If you wanna call her and hand me the phone, maybe I can straighten this thing out." His frustration had crept into his voice.

The woman stiffened and leaned away from him. "I'm sorry, but I can't do that. Linda isn't available right now. Why don't you have a seat, and we'll get this thing straightened out soon? What's your hurry? The race doesn't start for another three hours."

Max started to argue, but held back and let out a breath. This woman was right. What was his hurry?

Finally, he nodded and pulled out the metal folding chair next to her at the table. "I can't stay long."

She narrowed her eyes and studied him before she said, "You won't have to. We'll do whatever we can to fix this problem if you cooperate." There was a tension in her voice he hadn't heard earlier. Had he been responsible for that?

Since it was still so early, not many people came by the table to sign in. Max knew most of the runners would wait until the last minute, and the table would be surrounded by people all jogging in place. Max watched her as she smiled at each and every person who stopped. Her smile was genuine, he decided, and she was very well-liked by the people in this town. The only participants who seemed harried were those she didn't know, which made him think they must be from somewhere else.

Within ten minutes, Max knew her name. Patty. She had recently opened a business, he surmised, because nearly everyone asked her about it. And her business partner's name was Amy.

Max found himself wondering what kind of business she had. He assumed it must be a boutique or maybe even a hair salon. But when several men told her they were stopping by next week, he thought it might even be a real estate office.

Eventually, his curiosity got the best of him. He felt a strong desire to know what this woman did that so many people were interested in.

"You must have one heck of a business," Max said when there was a lull. "What is it you do?"

Patty looked at him, grinned, and actually turned a light shade of pink. Was she blushing?

"You might not believe me when I tell you," she said.

"Try me."

Chapter Two

Patty leaned away from the man named Max and got a good look at him. Was he seriously interested in what she did, or was he just making polite conversation? She'd noticed that his anger had softened after he was there a while.

From experience, Patty knew better than to share her enthusiasm with someone she wasn't sure about. Her excitement had been dampened so many times by people who didn't take her aspirations seriously because she was a woman in a world dominated by men. No, she'd play it cool with this one.

"I'm in the restoration business," she wound up saying.

His eyebrows arched. "Interesting. Old houses?"

"Not exactly," she said as she greeted the next runner. Hopefully, he'd forget this line of conversation by the time she signed this person up for the race.

No such luck. As soon as the runner left the table, Max turned to her with his arms folded across his chest.

"If it's not house restoration, then exactly what do you restore?" he asked, his voice almost challenging.

Patty couldn't think fast enough to divert his question. She knew she might as well come out and say it, even if he did start laughing.

"Car restoration," she blurted. Okay, so now he'd ask her what a woman like her was doing in the automotive business.

But he didn't. Instead, he slowly nodded, a grin creeping across his lips. "I like old cars. Do you specialize?"

Was he serious? Did he really want to know more about her business, or was he setting her up for a knockout? She might as well tell him more.

"Not really. I repair engines of classic automobiles. My partner and I just opened our shop six months ago." There. She'd said it. Now it was his turn to throw out a major put-down.

"You're an auto mechanic?" he asked, clearly surprised. His gaze wandered down from her face all the way to her running shoes. "You certainly don't look like any auto mechanics I've ever had before. Looks like things are really changing."

She wanted to lambaste him for making such a sexist comment, but she couldn't. There didn't seem to be a single hint of animosity or doubt in his voice when he'd made that comment. All the guys in Clearview respected her abilities in the garage, but they'd known her since they were children. In fact, she'd gotten into a few scrapes with many of them on the playground. New men almost never accepted what she did for a living, at first.

"You said you like old cars," Patty said. "Ever drive one?"

Max nodded. "Yes, as a matter of fact, I have an old Cadillac with me on this trip. I decided to take it on a drive through the country. It's my first two-week vacation in years." He'd leaned toward her with open interest.

"You're actually driving it?" Patty asked, amazed that someone would actually take an old car on such a long trip.

He shrugged. "That's what a car's for, isn't it? I know I'm putting mileage and wear and tear on it, but I figure I might as well have fun with my toys."

Patty found herself smiling at Max. Even though he'd initially come across as rude, his child-like spirit was showing through. Her friend Denise Carson Mitchell was like this, too. In fact, Patty remembered how Denise used to live for the day, with her devil-may-care attitude. And Denise was one of the few girls who'd accepted her for who she was. Looked like this man had the makings of a friend, after all.

Since there were so few people signing up early, Patty turned most of her attention to Max. She asked him questions about his car, and he replied with excitement. Patty found herself immersed in conversation when a familiar voice came up from behind.

"Patty, it's okay for you to leave now."

She jerked her head around and saw Linda. "Oh, hi, Linda." Patty stood, nearly knocking the metal folding chair over. Max reached out and righted it.

Linda glanced over at Max. "Are you a runner?"

Her puzzled expression prompted Patty to motion to Max. "I'd like you to meet Max. Max, this is Linda, the coordinator of the Clearview Cross Country Run."

Max stood and tilted his head toward Linda as he extended his right hand. "Nice to meet you, Linda. Patty and I were just talking cars."

Linda leaned back and belted out a hearty laugh. "Patty can talk cars all day. Now why don't the two of you run along and fill up on carbs. You'll need 'em for today."

"She's right," Max said. "Wanna get something to eat?"

Patty hesitated a few seconds before nodding. "Uh, sure, I'd like that."

Max grimaced and snapped his fingers. "We forgot something, Patty."

She thought for a moment, then she remembered. "Oh, yeah." Turning to Linda, she explained the situation about Max's name not being on the roster.

Linda didn't seem rattled in the least. "Let's go over the whole roster and see if we can find his name."

"I thought it was alphabetical," Patty said.

"It is, but you never know what might have happened. If we took his credit card number, we had to have gotten his name."

Patty took a step back as Linda handed the registration roster to Max. "Why don't you scan the list from the beginning and see if you can find your name while I get set up."

"I already looked over it once," he told her. "But I started with the D's."

Linda glanced back and forth between them and smiled. "Go over it again, only from the beginning. You might have missed something."

He nodded and began to peruse the list as he remained standing. Patty used this opportunity to study his features.

Max Dillard had a strong jaw, chiseled cheeks, and very dark hair. Almost black. In fact, he looked like he might be of Native American descent.

After several minutes of studying the list, his eyes twinkled and his lips twitched. "Billard?"

"What?" Linda said as she stood and looked over his shoulder. When she saw whatever it was she was looking at, she cackled. "No wonder you couldn't find it. Someone got your name wrong."

Patty looked at her. "I thought you were the one who took all the phone registrations."

48744

"Yeah," Linda said sheepishly. "I said someone got his name wrong. That someone was me." Then she turned to Max with an apologetic smile. "I'm really sorry."

"No problem." Max Dillard sounded much nicer now than he had in the beginning, Patty noticed.

Linda looked at the list again. "*Doctor* Dillard?"

He nodded. Patty tilted her head and looked at him again. He was a doctor?

"Or you may call me Dr. Billard if you want to," he said with a grin.

Linda laughed. "At least you have a sense of humor. Not everyone would take it so lightly."

"It's not worth getting upset about," he said. "Ready, Patty? I need some fuel for this race. Any doughnut shops around here?"

Patty felt Linda's curious gaze. She turned her head away from Linda and toward Max.

"How about a muffin?" Patty said. "There are some wonderful home-baked muffins in a little bakery on Main Street."

"You mean *healthy* muffins?" Max scrunched his nose.

"I don't know how healthy they are, but they're good, and they're homemade."

Max paused for a moment, pursed his lips, then nodded. Patty noticed that a smile kept threatening the corners of his mouth, so she didn't think he was too disappointed.

"Muffins are fine."

He bent over and tied his shoe, which gave Patty the opportunity to take another long look at him. *Doctor* Dillard? He didn't look like most doctors she knew. In fact, he looked way too young to have gone through medical school and established himself as a doctor. *He must be a lot older than he looks.*

"Mm," Max said, his eyes rolling back with a look of ecstasy. "These muffins are great."

"As good as a doughnut?"

With a chuckle, he replied, "Better."

They both took several bites before either of them spoke. For the first time since she could remember, Patty felt at ease with a man during a long period of silence. Max Dillard—*Doctor* Dillard—was a very comfortable man to be around, she was surprised to discover.

"Been running long?" he asked as he began to butter the second half of his muffin.

"I started running when I was little."

"Really? Are you doing it for health?"

"No," she said. "I'm doing it because I like it." She heard the irritation in her own voice, but that was how she felt. Why did most men think women had to have a reason to take up running? She'd heard it before. She was bracing herself for a battle between the sexes when he held up one finger.

"Sorry," he said as he began to pour a massive

amount of sugar into his coffee. "I have a tendency to stick my foot in my mouth. I didn't mean to offend you."

He apologized? Patty had been around men and boys all her life, but she rarely ever heard any of them apologize. The instant she thought that, she realized she was guilty of stereotyping just as much as she thought Max was.

"That's quite all right," she found herself saying to ease his mind, and hers as well, she realized. "Most women aren't raised by an auto mechanic father and two grease monkey brothers."

"How about your mom?" he asked innocently.

"She died when I was a little girl," Patty said as matter-of-factly as she could. She didn't want sympathy.

Max reached up and slapped a palm against his forehead. "I'm blowing it all over the place. Look, Patty, I'm really very sorry. Your past is none of my business."

Patty's heart twisted at his humility. "That's okay, Max. I was barely three when she died."

He shook his head and spoke softly. "That's so young to lose a mother. Do you miss her?"

She shrugged. "Not really because I have so few memories. Well, sometimes I think it would be nice to have a woman around who understood certain things I was going through. But since I never had a mom during those times, I learned how to figure things out on my own."

"With the help of those brothers of yours, right?"

"Yeah, if you wanna call it help,"

Max leaned back and laughed. "At least you dealt with it."

"I had no choice."

"Some people sit around feeling sorry for themselves when they're dealt a bad hand. But looks to me like you played the cards you got and did a good job of it." He paused and added, "You took the ball and ran with it."

Patty understood exactly what he was saying, since her brothers had talked sports all her life. "I enjoyed my childhood, though."

Max gestured widely with his hands. "Did you grow up here?"

"Yes. Clearview is a great place for children. Everyone knows you, or at least they did back when I was a kid. Things are starting to change, now that the town's growing."

"I noticed quite a few business buildings on the edge of town when I drove in. All that new?"

Patty nodded. "When I was younger, all we had were Main Street and a small strip mall about a mile away. Other than that, it was mostly neighborhoods, churches, parks, and schools."

"Sounds wonderful," he said. "Where I grew up, there were sidewalks, skyscrapers, and traffic."

"I bet that was exciting."

Max shook his head. "I guess it would have been if I'd been paying attention to what was going on around me. But I was too busy studying and getting through school."

"Oh, you were one of those, huh?" Patty said in a low tone.

His eyebrows shot up. "One of what?"

"The studious type."

"Yeah, I guess you could call me that."

"Have you always wanted to be a doctor?" she asked. And she really wanted to know. In fact, Patty wanted to know everything she could find out about this fascinating man who didn't seem the least bit put off by the fact that she was athletic and could handle herself in a traditionally male world.

"Yes, always," he replied. "But it's not exactly how I thought it would be."

"How's that?" she asked, wondering why he had such a somber expression.

"Somehow, I imagined myself healing sick people, taking care of children when they needed bones mended or fevers reduced."

"Isn't that what doctors do?"

Patty saw how Max had stopped eating his muffin and folded his hands on the table in front of him. Their conversation had touched a nerve, she could tell. But she was so curious she couldn't seem to stop.

"Maybe in Clearview," he told her, "but not where

I live. I mostly cater to people who want a pill for a quick fix and send the paperwork to their insurance companies."

He looked so sad, Patty wanted to reach out and comfort him, but she refrained. Touching his hand, as she itched to do, might be misconstrued.

"That's a shame," Patty said, holding one hand in the other to keep from making a move toward Max.

"Yes, it is," he said with a distant look in his eyes. Patty wondered what he was thinking.

They finished their muffins and coffee, Max dropped a couple of bills on the table, and they stood to leave. "It's time to get ready for the big race."

"Thanks for the muffin, Max," Patty said as she edged toward the door. "If you come back next year, I'll treat."

He grinned at her. "You're on."

Max watched Patty as she turned and jogged in the opposite direction from where he was headed. He'd never seen a woman so fast on her feet, yet so beautiful and poised, as Patty. She had a style he'd never seen in another woman, which attracted him much more than he was comfortable with. He hadn't been around many female athletes, other than a few runners who'd kept up with him in races over the years. And he hadn't taken the time to get to know any of them, so focused was he on his own performance.

After a long sigh, he headed toward his hotel. He

didn't have much to do to get ready for the race, but he figured he could change into his shorts and T-shirt, then do a little stretching. He'd finish warming up when he got back down to the street.

"Dr. Dillard," the desk clerk said as he walked into the hotel lobby. "I have a message for you." She reached below the desk and pulled out an envelope.

"Thanks." He turned toward the stairs. No sense in taking the elevator when he needed to warm up his muscles.

As soon as he got into his room, he tore into the envelope. It was from Linda at the Clearview Cross Country Run. It was another apology for her mistake. At the bottom she signed it, "Linda Johnson, President, Clearview Running Club."

Max was surprised Clearview had their own running club. But then he'd been surprised about a lot of things. Since he'd been here, he'd discovered a fabulous bakery, a quaint but cozy hotel, and a woman who could hold his interest for more than five minutes.

After he changed clothes and stretched for a few minutes, Max decided he was too antsy to hang around his hotel room any longer. Prolonged stays in enclosed spaces made him itch to escape. He grabbed his keys and left the room. Maybe there was something more interesting in town to keep him busy while he waited for the run to begin.

* * *

"Well?" Linda said when Patty finally returned to the booth after going home and changing into her new shoes. "What's he like?"

"What's who like?"

Linda rolled her eyes. "You know exactly who I'm talking about, Patty O'Neill. Don't play this game with me."

"Okay, okay," Patty said with a smile as she sat down in the vacant metal chair. "He's very nice." She folded her arms over her chest as she clamped her mouth shut and smiled.

"Is that all?"

Patty turned her head to keep her thoughts to herself for just a moment longer. She still wasn't sure what to think about Max Dillard, but she knew she was terribly attracted to him and that wasn't good.

Linda let out a long sigh. "Okay, Patty, have it your way. But I don't want you to choke in this race just because you have a crush on some cute doctor."

"Wait a minute," Patty blurted out in her own defense. "I don't have a crush on him. I just think he's really nice." Then she caught herself. "Okay, so I might have a little crush."

The smile on Linda's face was filled with sincere gladness. "There's nothing wrong with falling for a guy, Patty. Have you ever been in love?"

"Well, maybe not in *love*, but I did like a few guys back in high school, and maybe one really special guy in my shop class." Patty felt the rush of heat to her cheeks as she babbled.

"I'd say it's high time you met someone to fall head over heels for, then. And there's nothing wrong with starting with Max Dillard."

"You forgot one thing, Linda."

Leaning forward, Linda shook her head. "What's that?"

"He doesn't live in Clearview."

Chapter Three

"So? Lots of people date long distance," Linda continued, undaunted.

"It never works," Patty argued, as the idea of actually dating Max Dillard ran through her mind. She had to admit, it sounded pretty good to her, considering she hadn't had a date in months.

"Sure, it does. It just takes a little more effort, that's all."

"Well, I don't think it's gonna happen this time. I just met him today, and all we did was have muffins and coffee."

Linda's eyes darted away, causing Patty to turn around. There he was. Dr. Max Dillard, standing on the other side of the street, his running clothes showing enough of him to let her see he was in fabulous shape. Patty let out an audible sigh that caused Linda to turn back to her and smile.

"Yes," Linda said with appreciation, "he does look good."

Patty's face heated up. "Lots of guys look good."

"But not like this one." Linda raised her eyebrows. "Right?"

By now he'd crossed the street and was near enough to hear anything they said in normal voices. Patty forced herself to pretend indifference. She hoped she pulled it off.

"Don't let him get away," Linda whispered.

Patty didn't have a chance to say anything before he was standing beside them at the table. She suddenly felt like starting the race early, but she remained seated, plastered to the chair.

"Hi, Patty, I thought you might be here." Max hovered over her. *Oh, great.* Now her hands were beginning to sweat.

"Patty is such a big help at these races," Linda gushed. "Such a hard worker, and *everyone* loves her."

The forced smile on Patty's face actually hurt. She wanted to kick Linda under the table, but she remained cool.

Max grinned. "Yes, I can see why. She's a great lady."

They were talking about her as if she weren't there. "Okay, I've heard enough. Gotta run, Linda. Time to warm up." She tilted her head toward Max and studied him for a moment. Then, she stood up and bolted away from the table.

It was only a matter of seconds before she heard footsteps gaining on her. It was Max.

"Did I say something that upset you?" he asked. "Because if I did, I didn't mean it."

"No, of course you didn't. I just have to get my muscles warmed up. I haven't run in a while." Her tone was clipped, but she couldn't help it. How was she supposed to act right now?

"Then let's warm up together." The way Max said it left no room for her to argue.

Patty had a feeling Max spoke like that often, commanding attention and respect from everyone around him. This could be dangerous to her heart, she knew, so she needed to keep her emotional distance. However, at the moment, it was impossible to keep her physical distance, unless she wanted to be rude. And obvious. One thing her father had taught her was never to be rude. She didn't need lessons about not being obvious. She'd been born with that ability.

As they stretched their legs and torsos, Max spoke in even tones, asking her about past races. "Ever won this thing?"

"Once. Two years ago. I was in terrific shape back then, and we only had five hundred participants." *One, exhale, two. Don't forget to breathe, just because this great-looking guy is standing less than three feet away.*

"Looks to me like you're still in pretty good shape," he said without missing a beat. She felt the warmth of his gaze on her, but she willed herself not to look directly at him. "When was the last time you ran?"

"A couple of weeks ago," she replied.

Suddenly, Max straightened up, put his hands on his hips, and glared at her. "And you're running a marathon? Do you think this is a good idea, after not running for a couple of weeks?" He sounded way too much like an authority figure for her comfort. Must be the doctor part of him coming out.

Patty shrugged. "I should be okay as long as I warm up. My muscles are still pretty toned."

"You need to keep them conditioned, you know."

"Yes, I know. But I'll be careful."

The look on his face showed concern, which only endeared him more to Patty. She didn't want to feel this way about him, but she couldn't help it. He was quickly wedging his way into her heart, in spite of the fact that she'd put up as much guard as she could. Behind his gruffness was a sincere regard for her well-being.

Although she told herself it was strictly physical attraction she felt, she knew better. There were plenty of attractive men in Clearview, but none who made her insides churn the way Max did.

"If you start to cramp, you know you can stop, right?" he said, still staring at her.

"Yes," she replied, trying hard to sound annoyed

but not sure if she carried it off successfully. Instead of being bothered by his mother-hen attitude as she normally would, she liked it.

They stretched for several minutes in silence. Patty noticed the way his muscles tightened and then relaxed as he moved. She also saw how he looked at her with open admiration and appreciation.

"Ready?" he finally asked.

She nodded. It was time for the race to begin.

Patty was a knowledgeable runner. She understood that she needed to pace herself to be able to run the distance required to do well in this race. Having been out of condition for as long as she had, she harbored no delusions of actually winning the race. She just wanted to come in with a respectable time.

Max hung back with Patty, even though she knew he was capable of moving ahead of the pack. His breathing remained steady, even after she found herself panting.

"Don't overdo it, Patty," he said. "If you feel like stopping, no one will think any less of you."

She held her breath so he wouldn't hear her heavy breathing and smiled. Then she burst ahead of him.

As they turned the first corner, Patty felt a twitching sensation in her left calf. She slowed down just a little, and Max followed suit.

"Sure you're okay?" he asked.

"I'm fine," she snapped.

Shortly after that, her right leg began to twitch.

She'd finished less than one-fifth of the race, yet she was already starting to wear out. Now it was time for her mind to kick in and take over for her body. *Mind over matter.*

But no matter how many positive thoughts she forced into her brain, a slow, steady throbbing sensation began in Patty's legs. The pain intensified for the next few minutes, then her right leg starting tingling with numbness. She stumbled.

"Okay, I think you've had enough," Max told her, reaching out and touching her elbow.

She jerked her arm away. No way would she stop running now. This race only came once a year, and she wasn't about to give up so easily.

"I told you, I'm fine."

This time, when Patty tried to run faster, her legs wouldn't cooperate. She stumbled again, and before she knew what was happening, her knees slammed down hard on the pavement, nearly knocking the wind out of her.

The pain that flashed through Patty's lower extremities was so intense, she couldn't keep the tears from forming in her eyes. Biting her lip didn't help, either.

Without missing a beat, Max scooped her up into his arms and carried her off to the sidewalk, getting her out of the way of the runners behind them. He carefully set her down and then knelt down beside her.

"Go ahead, Max," she told him, her voice hoarse

with pain. "Finish the race. I'm fine. I'll just rest for a few minutes, and then I'll get back in."

"Oh, no, you don't," he told her. "You're finished for the day."

The tears continued to sting her eyes as she realized what he said was true. She was finished for the day. And she feared that she might be finished for good.

Ever since she'd opened her new business, Patty hadn't had the time she needed to stay in running shape. It took hours every week to keep her muscles toned and her lungs strong. But she was needed to repair the engines that her faithful customers trusted her with. She couldn't let them down. That was the difficult part about being responsible. Something had to give, and it had been her running.

Patty loved what she did. She felt fortunate to be able to follow her dream, but she also resented having to give up something else that was such an important part of her life. Her brother had told her it was impossible to do everything, and she knew he was right. But still, the thought of giving up running, even for her automotive business, filled her with a sense of dread.

"Looks like you've pushed beyond your limit," Max said after checking her out.

"No," she argued, "I just need a few minutes of rest. I'll be okay." *Just this one more race,* she reasoned to herself, *and I'll quit.*

"Oh, no, you don't. You're not going anywhere, if

I have to sit here and hold you down for the remainder of the race."

"But—"

He glared at her, stopping her words from coming. "If you don't want to do permanent damage, you'll be still."

Patty slowly nodded. She knew he was right. And she now felt responsible for holding him back from winning this race, which she was sure he could at the rate he was going.

"Why don't you go on ahead," she finally said as the reality of the situation settled over her.

"You sure?" he asked.

"Positive."

Max quickly glanced up, which made Patty turn around to see what he was looking at. Linda was coming up the sidewalk in a half walk, half run. She had the look of a mother tiger out to protect her cub, worry lines etched on her face.

"I heard you went down, Patty," Linda said as she sat next to Patty. "And I got here as fast as I could."

Patty let out a long sigh. "I wanted to finish this race so much I could taste it."

Max stood up with his hands on his hips, as if he wasn't sure whether to stay or leave. "You might need to hold her down. She's itching to get back up and run."

"Don't worry," Linda said reassuringly. "She's not going anywhere as long as I'm here."

"Thanks," Max said as he started to turn. But he stopped and moved toward Patty. "I want to talk to you tonight, if that's okay with you."

Patty nodded as she bit back the tears that still threatened to fall. "Okay." She would have agreed to anything to get him to turn away. Letting him see her cry would have shown her weakness, and she didn't want that.

"I'll call Linda to get your number when I'm done," he said, then he headed back for the group of runners.

"He's a pretty cool guy," Linda said as she reached down to inspect Patty's leg.

Patty flinched. "Yeah, he's pretty cool, except he threatened me if I tried to run again."

Linda froze. "He threatened you?"

"Well, not really. What he said was that he wouldn't finish the race if I acted like I might not cooperate."

A smile crept across Linda's face. "Smart man. We need a doctor like him in Clearview."

"We have all the doctors we need."

"Yeah, but most of them are five years or less from retiring."

"I'm sure someone will replace them."

"Wouldn't it be nice if Max was one of the replacements?" Linda asked in a teasing tone.

Patty tried to move, but Linda's firm hand was still on her shoulder. As long as she was there, Patty knew she couldn't get back in the race. She was definitely finished for the day.

"Yeah, but highly unlikely to happen."

"Maybe so, but we can always let him know this town needs someone like him."

It took almost an hour before Patty could stand. Linda offered to call an ambulance, but Patty refused, saying she'd rather crawl back home than be taken to the hospital in the back of an ambulance. The image of her mother being taken away was still the most vivid memory Patty had of her, and Linda was sensitive to that.

Patty let Linda drive her home, then she hobbled into her house. The instant she got inside, she grabbed the arms of her furniture and used them to make her way to the sofa, where she flopped in a heap. She was beginning to hurt all over now, her back stiff and her legs still cramping.

Everything that had happened over the past several months had seemed almost too good to be true. She'd met Amy at the car show, Amy had offered to become her business partner, and then she'd been surprised to learn that Amy had enough capital to keep them out of debt. They were able to hit the ground running with Classic Cars, complete with Amy's new knowledge of interior repair. And as if that hadn't been enough, Amy had a great mind for business.

Patty felt like she'd fallen into a gold mine. But the one thing she'd sacrificed—her running—had put the crimp in the picture.

She loved running. Always had. When she was a

little girl, Patty used to take things from her brothers' rooms to get them to chase her. Then she'd run as fast as her little legs would carry her, teasing and taunting them to keep them chasing her. This lasted for years before they realized it was a game with her. Then, she'd had to find another way to get her adrenaline pumping hard enough to run fast.

In high school, Patty discovered track. She ran both short and long distances, something no other girl had been able to do. Her school records still stood, which made her beam with pride every time she went to a high school athletic function. Her name was engraved on a plaque by the gym.

Since most of what Patty did was tomboyish, she didn't have a lot of girlfriends in school. When she was in elementary and junior high school, girls teased her and called her boy names. In high school, they became a little more civil toward her, but she'd still felt like an outcast.

Linda had been a grade ahead of her. They'd become friends when Patty had repaired Linda's car's engine in the senior parking lot after school. None of the other kids, including the boys, knew anything about engines, but Patty did. She spotted the problem right away, and with a few simple tools had Linda on her way. Linda never forgot that, and they'd been friends ever since.

This opened many doors for Patty, since Linda was quite a popular girl. Linda was never without a date on weekends, and she was always laughing and giggling with her friends. Linda started to include Patty in some of her social activities, and over the years that had never changed. Linda was loyal to a fault, something Patty was grateful for.

Two hours after Patty got home, her phone rang. She carefully stood up, making sure her legs didn't buckle beneath her, and moved gingerly over to the phone. It was Gertie Chalmers, Bethany Hadaway's grandmother, the woman who loved to take care of everyone in Clearview who was younger than she, which covered more than ninety-five percent of the population.

"I heard you took a spill in the race, Patty," Gertie barked. "Whatever possessed you to run with all you've got going on?"

Patty relaxed at the sound of Gertie's voice. Gertie had been there many times when she just needed someone to talk to. There was no way she could ever be mad at this caring soul.

"I have no idea, Gertie. I thought I was in good enough shape to do it, though, or I would never have tried." Patty had to sit down on the chair beside the phone, her legs still felt so weak.

"Obviously, that's not the case. I just hope it doesn't prevent you from doing your job at the shop."

"Don't worry, Gertie, I won't forget about your car."

Gertie drove one of the oldest cars in town, and

although it wasn't yet a classic, Patty suspected it would be someday, based on how well Gertie maintained it.

"Don't worry about my car. It's you and your livelihood I care about."

Patty had no doubt this was the case. Gertie sincerely cared about everyone she took under her wing.

"Look, I didn't call you to fuss at you, although heaven knows you need a good tongue-lashing," Gertie said in her typical brisk tone. "I was just wondering if you wanted to stop by my old house tomorrow afternoon and have a picnic in the back yard."

Gertie was true to form, inviting the injured over for a meal. Patty knew she'd been accepted by the people of Clearview when she was invited over to Gertie's old house, where Bethany and Reverend David Hadaway lived. David had bought the house from Gertie a few years ago, and he told his new grandmother-in-law that she could come over any time she wanted. Gertie took him up on his offer more often than he'd probably intended. Patty had never once seen David flinch. He always took things in stride, which was an admirable trait in a preacher.

"What time?" Patty asked as she shifted to get into a more comfortable position.

"About one. We probably won't eat until two, but you might want to come hang out with us."

"Will Jonathan be there?" Patty asked. Jonathan was David's nephew, who seemed to be with David and

Bethany more than he was with his own parents, who'd had marital problems for as long as Patty had known them.

"Of course he will," Gertie said. "Gotta have a young 'un around to keep things interesting."

Patty laughed. "You got that right. Sure, I'll be there. What can I bring?"

"Normally, I'd tell you to bring a salad, but since you're hurt, don't worry about it. Just bring yourself."

"Thanks, Gertie." Patty wasn't about to go empty-handed, but she didn't argue. She knew better.

"Any time." Gertie sucked in a breath, a warning that there was more. "Oh, and Patty, don't worry about how you're gonna get there. I have someone picking you up, since I figured you might have a little trouble driving with those injured legs of yours."

Patty felt a tingling sensation on the back of her neck. Gertie was up to something, she could tell.

"Who?"

"Don't worry about it," Gertie said.

"I want to know who's picking me up," Patty said, trying to demand an answer.

"If a nice-looking young man in a beautiful old Cadillac pulls up in front of your house, you'll know it's for you," Gertie replied.

After they got off the phone, Patty remained sitting in the chair for a few minutes. How in the world did Gertie do it? Since Patty had lived in Clearview all her life, she knew what everyone drove. And the only nice-looking young man who drove an old Cadillac she knew about was Max. She had a feeling Linda had something to do with this.

A phone call to Linda didn't reveal much, though. "What're you talking about, Patty?"

"I'm talking about Gertie Chalmers. She invited me to Bethany's and David's house tomorrow for a picnic."

"How nice," Linda said. "Gertie sure does know how to host a party."

"Yes, but what do you know about it?"

"Well, she invited me, too."

"Anyone else that you know of?" Patty asked, wishing she could see Linda's face.

"Uh, sure. There are a few other people."

Sucking in a breath and blowing it out in exasperation, Patty continued her interrogation. "Does one of those people happen to be Dr. Max Dillard?"

"Well . . . maybe."

"Maybe?" Patty shrieked. "Are you saying you're not sure?"

"No, I'm not saying that."

"Then what are you saying?"

Linda cleared her throat and began talking very quickly, her voice cracking every few words. "Max called me right after the race. By the way, did I tell you he came in third? Anyway, he said he was worried about you, and he wanted to know how you were doing. I just happened to run into Gertie at the grocery

48 *Debby Mayne*

store on my way home, and I told her what had happened to you. She said she wanted to do something to help." With Linda firing her words so rapidly, Patty didn't have a chance to interrupt.

Finally, when she heard Linda slow down, Patty said, "How did Max get into the picture?"

"When Gertie asked who the winners were, I told her how Max had stopped to help you and he still came in third. Isn't that awesome, Patty?"

"Yes," Patty agreed, "it is awesome." She also knew that if it weren't for stopping to help her, Max probably would have won the race. She felt awful. A race like this was important to an avid runner.

"One thing led to another, and then Gertie said she'd like to meet Max. I thought it might be a good idea, since we're thinking about asking him to move here."

That last comment got Patty's attention. "Who's thinking about asking Max to move here?"

"Remember? We were talking about it today."

"We weren't serious," Patty argued.

"Maybe you weren't, but I was. Just think about it, Patty. Wouldn't it be great to have a new doctor in town? Maybe we wouldn't have to wait a week to get an appointment. One additional doctor will make a huge difference in a town this small."

Patty was overwhelmed from Linda's tirade. "Whatever. Just don't say anything to him until we have a chance to talk about it first."

She could practically hear Linda smiling over the phone. "Okay, whatever you want me to do. But don't put it off too long. Max has to get back to the city in two weeks."

"He's not gonna be here the whole two weeks, though," Patty told her.

"He might."

"Max told me he was going to drive through the country and stop in small towns off the interstate."

"Perhaps he's changed his mind," Linda said with a hint of something secretive in her voice. Patty was generally suspicious of Linda, but now she knew her friend must have something up her sleeve.

"Linda," she said slowly, giving the phone the most menacing look she could manage.

"Hey, don't worry about it."

Patty could imagine how much effort it took Linda not to smile. Yep, Linda was definitely up to something.

She got off the phone wondering if she should be glad that Linda would be at the Hadaways' house. Normally, she would, but it appeared that her friends might be ganging up on her. They were definitely ganging up on Max. She wondered how he'd handle it.

Chapter Four

The people in this town sure were friendly, Max thought as he showered and changed into his street clothes. And they all seemed disappointed he hadn't won the race.

He was disappointed, too, but it couldn't be helped. Patty had taken a fall, and she needed him.

Max felt his chest squeeze. Someone had actually needed him. She'd needed not only his medical skills but his strength to carry her to safety. It felt good. And she'd never once asked for a pain pill. This was new for Max.

All the money and prestige of his family's medical practice didn't hold a candle to being truly *needed*. For the first time since he'd been out of medical school, Max had the feeling of accomplishing something he'd been trained to do.

Sure, he'd handed out prescriptions for headaches, stomach aches, and other pains his patients had. And once in a while he had to set a broken bone when someone fell off his horse during a game of polo or broke a wrist during an overly ambitious racquetball match. But this was different. It was getting down to reality and what people truly needed, rather than catering to pampered people who just wanted a quick fix.

If he weren't so deeply involved in the family practice, Max might even think about doing what that sweet but feisty elderly woman who'd introduced herself as Gertie had jokingly suggested. Moving to Clearview was definitely something that appealed to him. But he couldn't. Maybe he could have considered it a few years ago, but not now.

The people in this town were incredibly amiable. People he'd never even seen before had hugged him after he'd carried Patty to safety. It was clear that the folks in Clearview cared for their own and that they considered him a hero for rescuing a damsel in distress.

Max had to laugh at that thought. Patty O'Neill a damsel in distress? Hardly!

That woman was an enigma, from the way she carried herself like a beauty pageant queen to her athletic ability. And she was an auto mechanic to boot. That would shock even the most open-minded man.

Then he frowned. Her muscles had cramped up on her pretty badly. He'd seen people become incapacitated for days and even weeks after stressing muscles that hadn't been worked. What if it affected her business? Could she handle that?

Max wasn't sure, but he suspected this was her only source of income. He'd have to really listen tomorrow to find out if there was any kind of need he could help with further.

When Gertie had asked him to the picnic, his first reaction was to turn her down. After all, he hadn't planned to stick around town all day. His vacation had just started, and he wanted to see some of the countryside.

But after hearing that Patty would be there, suddenly the picnic sounded like a very interesting plan. He wanted to see her again.

Maybe he should try to see her tonight. After all, she'd agreed to talk to him after the race. Besides, she needed him, he thought with a smile. He felt a soft glow as the very idea of taking care of Patty crossed his mind.

Linda had given him Patty's phone number. He pulled it out of his wallet and looked at it. Maybe he should just call to check up on her, then go out to dinner by himself.

No, that didn't sound good. He wanted to spend a

little more time with Patty. Maybe if he did that, he'd get her out of his system and she'd be just a momentary diversion for him. He seriously doubted that would happen, but he could hope.

After memorizing Patty's phone number, he moved over to the hotel room phone. He'd know pretty quickly if she was up to going out to dinner with him.

She answered on the second ring.

"How ya feeling?" he asked, trying hard to keep his voice from showing what he felt.

"A little sore, but much better." Her voice sounded strained, so he knew she was trying to hide her discomfort. She obviously wasn't a whiner.

"Hungry?"

"Um, I guess I am, just a little," she replied. "I haven't had anything to eat since the muffin this morning. Why?"

Max did some quick thinking, then decided he'd take a chance. "I was thinking I could do one of two things. Either I can come and get you and we can go out to dinner, or if you're not up to it, I can pick something up and bring it to you."

"You'd do that?" She sounded stunned.

"Yes, I would. In fact, I insist. Where can I get carry-out around here?"

Patty laughed, and he suddenly felt stupid. "What's so funny about that?"

"Well, there's the Burger Barn. And there's Mc-Donald's and Burger King. Or if you want pizza, we have a few new chain restaurants on the other side of town."

"No Chinese?" he asked. Clearview was definitely a small town that could use a few more conveniences.

"Not yet, but I'm sure when someone realizes what we're missing, we'll have it soon." Her voice sounded much lighter now, probably because she found his questions so amusing.

"Which sounds better to you?" he asked. "Burger Barn or McDonald's?"

"That's a tough decision, but since you're not from here, you might as well try some of our local cuisine. Burger Barn."

Max chuckled. "Tell me what you want and where it is, and I'll bring it to your house. Oh, you need to give me your address, too."

He heard another brief hesitation before she gave him the information he asked for. After writing it all down and verifying what she wanted, he hung up. His mood was soaring, now that he knew he'd be seeing Patty again soon.

As he approached her house, Max noticed that the neighborhood was filled with small, cottage-style houses, unlike anything he was accustomed to. But it was nice. Very homey.

Patty was standing at the door waiting for him. He reached over and grabbed the sacks filled with chili cheese dogs and onion rings, then quickly moved toward her.

"You need to get off your feet, or your muscles never will heal," he said in his professional voice.

"Doctor's orders?" she asked with a lifted brow.

With a crisp nod, Max said, "That's right. Now sit down, and I'll put the food on plates."

She led him to a kitchen that was bright and cheery. The walls were a pale blue, and the curtains on the window above the sink matched perfectly.

"Nice color scheme," he said. "Blue is my favorite color."

"Mine, too," Patty said. "Back when I was in elementary school, and all the other little girls wore pink ruffles and lace, I had on my brothers' hand-me-downs. And I probably don't have to tell you nothing was pink. It was all blue, green, and black."

Max studied her to see if there was any remorse, but he didn't detect any. She seemed perfectly content with her lot in life, something he couldn't say about most people.

"Plates?" he asked, looking around. If he knew her better, he would have started opening cabinets in search of something to put their food on.

She went to the pantry and came back with two paper plates. "I'm not into heavy duty clean-up from the Burger Barn. We can just toss these when we're done."

Max liked this. It was like having a picnic inside. That reminded him.

"I hope you don't mind if I'm at the picnic tomorrow. That sweet old lady wouldn't take no for an answer."

Patty held up one finger. "First rule in Clearview: Never argue with Gertie Chalmers. You're wasting your time if you do. When she tells you something, just do it. You'll wind up doing whatever she wants anyway, so there's no point in wasting time."

He chuckled. "Mrs. Chalmers sounds like quite a woman."

"Oh, she is. In fact, I think she considers everyone in town to be like a grandchild. She meets no strangers."

Max felt honored to have met Gertie. "I'm really looking forward to tomorrow." He smiled openly at her.

Patty froze for an instant and looked at him, almost as if she needed to see if he was serious. Then she smiled back. "Me, too."

Max cleared his throat to cover the emotions that welled inside his chest. He knew he really shouldn't allow himself to feel anything beyond friendship toward Patty, but he was afraid that was impossible now. His attraction to her was growing by the second.

The woman across the table from him kept the conversation going, never once mentioning the pain he knew she must be feeling. Her muscles had taken a beating this morning, and unless she was taking serious pain medication, she had to still feel it. But she didn't show any signs of being medicated. Her conversation was clear, and she was totally coherent.

When his curiosity got the best of him, Max brought up her condition. "How are your legs?"

"My legs?" she said, grimacing for the first time since he'd seen her this time. She shrugged. "I guess they're okay."

"Hurting?"

"Maybe a little. But I'll be fine."

"You really need to stay off your feet as much as possible, Patty. Those muscles need to heal. I have a feeling you might have seriously strained them, and they won't get better unless you take care of yourself."

Patty put her chili cheese dog down on the paper plate in front of her. She leaned forward and looked directly at him.

"Max, I don't have the luxury of staying off my feet. I'm a working woman who has never asked anyone to do a thing for me. That will continue, even when I'm hurt. Understand?"

He swallowed hard. She sure was being defensive. "Yes, I understand. It's just that I'm concerned."

She softened a little as she continued. "And I appreciate your concern, but there's a strong reality here. I live alone, in case you didn't notice, and I have to fend for myself. On Monday, I have to be back at work fixing cars. Sure, my legs will probably hurt, but once I get inside a car engine, I'll forget all about the pain. One thing that keeps my mind off pain is doing what I love to do."

Max sat back with a start. She'd just laid it on the line for him. She was passionate—about her work and about the fact that she didn't need anyone telling her what to do. And he found himself falling for her even more. This wasn't good.

"Can you take short breaks and get off your feet throughout the day?" he asked, taking the chance that she might bite his head off.

"Sometimes," Patty replied, giving him no indication of anger. "All depends on what I have waiting for me when I get there. Sometimes I have time to open the mail and plan a schedule. Other times, I have three cars lined up for emergency repairs."

"Need some help?" he asked. "I've done some light automotive work in the past." Max couldn't believe what he was offering, but he couldn't just leave Patty when she needed someone to help.

Her head tilted to one side as an expression of disbelief covered her face. "I thought you were a doctor."

"I am, but I know a little about cars. I can change oil, and if there's an obvious problem with the engine, I might be able to help diagnose." He looked down, then back into her eyes. "Oh, and I can change fan belts, too."

Her smile hit him like a thunderbolt. Patty O'Neill had the fullest lips, the widest smile, the brightest eyes, and the highest cheekbones he'd ever seen. She was drop-dead gorgeous, and the biggest bonus of all was that it didn't seem to matter to her. In fact, he wasn't even sure if she realized just how good she looked.

"I thought you were leaving for vacation after the race," Patty said slowly.

"That's what I thought, too, but I'm having too much fun here."

Patty licked her lips and nodded. She looked like she was thinking hard about something, and he didn't want to interrupt her. He found himself eagerly anticipating her response to his offer.

When she nodded, his heart hammered. "If you really want to stay, I might be able to use your help."

"Really?" he said, realizing the instant the word came out of his mouth that he sounded too eager. It even surprised him a little.

Nodding, Patty replied, "A couple of my clients need simple things like oil changes and lube jobs. Even the cars that need more extensive work could use oil changes, too." Her smile vanished as a look of horror crossed her face. "I'm sorry, Max, I didn't mean to take advantage of your offer. It's just that—"

He reached over and gently placed two fingers over her mouth, shushing her. Her eyes widened.

Max smiled at her. She was truly unique. Most women he knew back home didn't think twice at the idea of taking advantage of him. In fact, they seemed to pride themselves in it. He couldn't imagine any of them apologizing for taking him up on his offer.

"This is something I really want to do. You're not taking advantage of me."

"You sure?"

"Positive." Max wiped his mouth with his napkin and pushed back from the table. "That food was fabulous."

"It was, wasn't it?" Patty agreed. She looked at Max in wonder. She'd always liked the Burger Barn, but the food he brought tasted even better than it normally did. It had to be because he was sitting across the table from her.

Her first impression of him was that he was arrogant and demanding. It didn't take long to realize she was wrong.

This man was generous to a fault, and she hated the idea of making him feel responsible for her welfare. So far, Patty had never had to depend on anyone in her adult life, and she wasn't about to start now. Her father and brothers had taught her to take care of herself, something she valued considerably. She didn't want to lose that ability.

"Would you like dessert?" she asked.

Max shrugged. "I started to get one of the desserts at the Burger Barn, but I didn't think the ice cream would survive the trip."

"No, you're probably right. Their ice cream is good,

but it's best eaten there. But I have some brownies Gertie brought over a few days ago."

"Brownies?" he asked. "Sounds great."

Max helped her get the platter of brownies, two glasses, and a carton of milk. Patty enjoyed the domesticity of this whole situation, which bothered her. No one had ever accused her of being domestic, and she didn't think it would be a good idea to cultivate that image now.

"This is fun," Max told her.

"Fun?" She paused and glanced at him over her shoulder.

"Yeah," he replied. "I can't remember ever having this much fun just hanging out and chatting with a lady. You're easy to talk to."

Patty turned back around and finished getting the dessert plates down from the shelf. Did he mean that as a compliment? Or was he letting her know that being with her was like being with one of the guys? To her dismay, that wasn't what she wanted. She wanted Max to see her as a woman. Someone he could imagine holding in his arms. Someone he could dream of kissing and expressing undying love for.

Suddenly, her brain kicked in. What was she thinking? Undying love? No way! That was the last thing she needed at this time in her life—especially with someone from out of town. Long-distance relationships never worked, except in movies.

"Hey, Patty," Max said with a gentleness no man

had ever shown her. "What's wrong? Did I say something?"

She forced a smile. "No, nothing's wrong. I just have a lot on my mind." He wouldn't understand.

"I can imagine, now that you've got such a demanding business going. I remember when I first went into practice with my family. There was so much to remember, I felt like I needed to shut out everything else."

Maybe he *did* understand. "Well, now that you mention it, I do have a lot to think about. I'm afraid I might have taken on more than I should have, just a little too fast."

Max propped his elbows on the table and appeared to be making himself comfortable. And she felt like he was very open to anything she wanted to discuss. Maybe she should talk with him about it. After all, he was only in town for a little while. Nothing would ever get past him, unless he suddenly became talkative tomorrow at the picnic, which she thought would be highly unlikely since Denise would be there. It was hard to get a word in edgewise around her.

Nodding, Max said, "If you tell me what's going on, I might have a few suggestions."

She began by explaining how she'd put ads in several antique auto magazines. "It seemed like a good idea at the time. But what I found was that there are so few people who want to specialize in cars thirty years old or older, I had more than I could handle.

Most mechanics do that kind of work in their spare time."

"So you've been flooded with requests for engine repairs?" he said, urging her to continue.

"Yes. And I haven't been able to turn anyone down, either."

"Why not?"

"In the beginning," she went on, "it didn't seem like a good idea to turn any business away. But then, after a couple of months of twelve-hour days, I thought I might want to take a step back. Amy's my business partner, and she said we could afford to take half the customers who call and still have enough money for the salaries we get."

Max held up his hands in confusion. "Then what's the problem?"

She felt like all her energy was slowly creeping out of her body as she talked. "The car shows in this area really need someone who knows what they're doing. I've enlisted the help of Amy's husband, Zach. He's really good, but he still has his regular business to deal with."

"So what you're saying is that you don't want to let anyone down, right?" Max said softly.

Patty bit her lip and nodded. "I suppose that's one way of putting it."

"You remind me of my mother," he said with a chuckle.

"What?" she shrieked. His mother? What was that supposed to mean?

"Whoa, Patty, calm down. My mother's a really cool woman. It's just that she has a hard time saying no to anyone she thinks might need her. And people love to take advantage of that wonderful quality. I have a feeling this is what's happening to you. You've probably always followed through on all your promises, and people know that. That's why they come to you, begging."

A rush of air left Patty's lungs. "Yeah, you're right again. How did you know all this about me? Did Gertie tell you?"

Patty remembered Gertie having the same talk with her a couple months after she'd started the business. One afternoon when they'd crossed paths on Main Street, Gertie had stopped, turned, and told Patty to stop right where she was. Then, Patty got the biggest lecture she could ever remember getting about not letting people run all over her.

With two brothers who loved to tease her, she'd never thought she was easily used. But now she knew she was kidding herself: she was a pushover.

"No, Gertie didn't tell me," Max said with tenderness. "But it's pretty obvious, based on what you've said. Why don't you have someone else accept new clients?"

Patty shook her head. "I can't do that. I have to look at all the cars that come in. No one else knows the engines as well as I do." As soon as she said that, she regretted it. "That sounded pretty pompous, didn't it?"

"Not really," Max replied. "I have a feeling you're the best mechanic around here who specializes in classic cars. But one person can only do so much."

"You sound like you're talking from experience."

Slowly, Max nodded. "I am."

Chapter Five

Patty tilted her head and stared at the man in front of her for a moment before responding. "Do you have a hard time turning people down, too?"

Max nodded. "I used to."

"What happened?" It was important for Patty to know. This affliction had been with her all her life, but she'd kept it to herself. It wasn't until recently that other people had noticed.

"Several of the patients who came to see my grandfather were upset when he retired. They were assigned to me." Max stopped for a moment to catch a breath. "At first, I thought everything would be just great. I figured all the patients would welcome me with open arms and accept me, simply because I was a doctor."

Patty smiled. Even she knew that couldn't happen.

He went on. "Instead of being happy about their new young doctor, people began to grumble. So what I did was what any self-respecting, fresh-out-of-med-school doctor would do."

"What's that?"

"I worked night and day trying to earn their respect and confidence. Never once did I make people wait more than a day or two for an appointment. If I was booked, I just added another hour to my day."

"Did you get what you wanted?" Patty asked.

"Let's just put it this way. I got what I *thought* I wanted."

"Explain," Patty said bluntly. She'd never been one for excess words.

Max leaned toward her, making her pulse take off like a jackhammer. "What I thought I wanted was to keep all my grandfather's patients and then pick up a few of my own. I wanted to be the perfect doctor, curing every single ailment that came through the office doors. And I didn't ever want to make a mistake because, after all, I was the doctor, and I was supposed to be in control."

"Then what happened?" Patty asked. She knew he'd only told her half the story.

"First of all, in spite of my efforts, a handful of my grandfather's patients found another doctor, someone who wasn't quite so young. And the ones I managed to keep expected the same level of care—or should I say coddling—forever. I couldn't do it and stay sane. I had to take some time off."

"Yes, I can see where that would be a problem," Patty said. "So how did you deal with it?"

Max shrugged. "I started keeping regular office hours rather than staying until the last person wanted an appointment. Of course, I take care of emergencies, and I have my two days a week when I'm on call twenty-four hours. But at least I have a portion of my life back."

As the dawning of understanding flooded Patty's mind, she let out a heavy sigh. "That's all behind you, and you know how it turned out. But what about my business? Is it too soon to turn people away?"

"Not really."

"What if they think I can't handle the work?"

"They won't think that, Patty," Max reassured her. "In fact, you might find that it has the total opposite effect. People will probably call way in advance and schedule regular maintenance appointments in order to make sure they get their cars worked on by the best mechanic around."

She chewed her lip for a moment as she thought about it. What Max said made sense. But it still made her a little nervous. She'd have to discuss it with Amy.

"Hey, Patty, let's lighten up and talk about tomorrow." Max's eyebrows were raised, and he looked at her with compassion.

With a grin, Patty said, "Okay, so what do you wanna know?"

"Something about the people who'll be there. I already know Gertie and Linda. How about Gertie's granddaughter and her family?" He leaned back in his chair, folded his arms, and waited.

Patty told him all about the people she'd grown close to over the past several months. She'd known them all her life, but it wasn't until she'd befriended Amy that she'd become part of their inner circle. It wasn't that they were intentionally leaving her out in the past. In fact, it was more because they thought she didn't have time for them, since she was always playing sports or had her head under the hood of a car.

Gertie's granddaughter, Bethany, had been best childhood friends with Denise, who'd married Amy's brother. Bethany owned a bookkeeping service, and her husband was the pastor of the most popular and youthful church in town. Their daughter's name was Emily. David's nephew Jonathan spent most weekends and holidays at their home because it was a much happier place than his own home, where his parents were always on the verge of divorce.

Denise was the sole proprietor of the only bookstore in Clearview, and her husband, Andrew, was national sales manager of a gift wrap company. They had recently sold their mansion in the most exclusive neighborhood in Clearview and purchased a more modest home in a newer section of town. Denise loved to putter in the yard when she wasn't at her bookstore, so the front of her house was like a kaleidoscope of color, mirroring her personality. Flowers in every hue bloomed across the front of her house.

Amy and Zach had purchased the house Denise lived in when she was single, and they seemed perfectly happy in the tiny cottage. Amy once told her she'd never lived in a house so small, and she'd never felt so free to enjoy life. Living in Clearview certainly agreed with her.

"They sound like a nice bunch of people," Max said when she wound down. "I'm just wondering why they invited me."

Patty had wondered the same thing, but the more she thought about it, the more she realized that Max Dillard would fit in. And the more suspicious she became.

Linda was already starting to send signals that they'd been talking about working on getting Max to move his practice to Clearview. That was the most ridiculous thing Patty had ever heard. They'd just met him. Besides, what doctor in his right mind would want to just pick up and leave a thriving family practice?

"Probably because they like you," Patty told him.

"They don't know me well enough to know if they like me," he told her.

"You saved me, didn't you?"

He laughed. "I wouldn't put it that way, but I can see where they might think that."

"There you go, then." Patty leaned back and allowed herself to take in the vision sitting across the table from her. To have been rescued by a man like that was almost unbelievable.

Never in her wildest dreams did Patty ever think she'd meet a man like Max. Not only was he handsome, smart, and humble, he was fun to be around. Plus, he didn't seem intimidated by her in the least.

After they chatted for a few more minutes, Max stood up. "I really need to leave now. I don't want to wear out my welcome."

Patty started to tell him he wasn't wearing out his welcome and that she loved having him in her house. But she clamped her mouth shut and didn't say anything. She just nodded. Even as inexperienced with men as she was, she knew better than to sound too eager.

"You don't have to walk me to the door," he told her. "I know the way out."

Ignoring what he said, Patty followed him to the door, hobbling. "I hope you don't get indigestion from the Burger Barn," she said with a smirk.

"Trust me," Max said as he leveled her with his gaze, "it takes a whole lot more than a meal at the Burger Barn to give me indigestion."

Then he got in his car and took off. The Cadillac had been well maintained. Patty could tell from the way it sounded when he started the engine. And vintage cars like that didn't come cheap. She itched to get her hands on the engine to see how it looked. But she made a promise to herself right then and there that she wouldn't ask.

Patty's legs felt like they'd been filled with lead when she awoke on Sunday morning. She carefully swung them around, put her feet on the floor beside her bed, and reached down to massage her calves before attempting to stand.

She'd been an athlete for a long time and she'd had to deal with soreness before, but this was the worst she could remember. It was also the least conditioned she'd ever been before a marathon run. She should have known better.

As soon as she felt like her legs could bear her weight, she carefully made her way into the kitchen, holding onto the backs of furniture along the way. Each step shot a sharp pain through her, but she just winced and went on.

Two cups of coffee later, Patty stood up from the kitchen table and tried walking again. To her surprise, the pain wasn't quite as intense as it had been when she'd first awakened. A warm bath would help.

Fortunately, Patty was an early riser, so she had plenty of time to soak her legs and still get ready for church, something she'd started going to when she became friends with Denise and Bethany. At first, she told herself it was to show support for Bethany's husband David, but she eventually admitted she loved being there. Not only were David's sermons interesting, she enjoyed being surrounded by her new group of friends. For the first time in her life, she felt like she belonged, and she wanted to bask in the warmth of what they provided.

Each step after the bath became easier, until she had to remind herself to take it easy. Working the muscles was good, but overdoing it would send her to the floor in pain.

Patty wore a simple shift-style dress in her favorite color, blue. She knew she looked good in this color, but the dress was so plain, she had to wear more accessories. Instead of wearing the ponytail she preferred at work, she left her hair hanging straight, parted on the side. Sometimes it annoyed her, but Amy had convinced her she looked very feminine, and this was what she wanted. The sacrifice of comfort was well worth the compliments she received.

There was still ample parking in the church lot, since Patty had arrived early. She wound her way toward some shade, and this was when she spotted Max's car. In fact, there was no missing the huge, shiny tail fins that were the trademark of the Cadillac.

Her heart thudded as she contemplated turning around and heading back home. She hadn't been prepared for seeing Max at church, although now that she thought about it, she should have known he'd be invited. Gertie was the town social director, and she always took it upon herself to get people to church on Sunday. No doubt Reverend David Hadaway appreciated her efforts, since he was enjoying banner numbers in attendance.

Max sat on the edge of the pew, glancing back every time he heard the double doors swish open. He tried to fool himself into thinking he was curious about this small-town church and its friendly people. But he knew what he was looking and listening for. Patty O'Neill.

Hopefully, she wouldn't notice how eager he was to see her. It would probably scare her away.

Ever since meeting Patty, his mind had taken on a whole new pattern of thoughts. Before, all he could think about was getting rest before returning to the drudgery of his medical practice.

Now, though, his idea of a great vacation was hanging out in Clearview, eating at the Burger Barn, and seeing Patty every chance he got. No one he knew would believe this.

He'd given a little thought to what would happen if he was actually free to move here. It sounded promising for the right person, even if it couldn't possibly be him.

His head swam with confusion over this issue. One minute, Max actually thought it might work. Then the next minute, he realized it was next to impossible.

First of all, he couldn't leave his family with more regular patients than they could handle—not with a brand-new doctor who needed guidance. And second, why would he think he could move to Clearview just because he'd spent a fabulous couple of days? Brand-new doctors didn't always garner the respect he already enjoyed back home. Or was that truly respect?

Max absentmindedly glanced over his shoulder when the doors opened again. He did a double-take when he caught a glimpse of Patty.

Man, she was absolutely drop-dead gorgeous—even more beautiful than when he'd first laid eyes on her. Her blue dress was framed across the top by her cascading hair, highlighted by sparkling silver jewelry. Women back home paid big bucks for a face like that.

Max's palms began to sweat as he turned to face the front, then looked back at Patty in a quick, nervous gesture. He wasn't sure where to look, so he forced himself to stare at the empty pulpit before allowing himself another peek at her.

Slowly, he turned his head and found himself sharing a gaze with the woman in blue. There might as well not have been anyone else in the room. Her eyes widened, then her lips parted as she smiled back at him.

Was he smiling? Now that he thought about it, he sure was! It was probably the stupidest grin she'd ever seen. He quickly licked his lips and motioned for her to join him.

She hesitated for a split second, then continued her forward momentum toward him. He watched her walk and wondered how she managed to be so graceful on those heels after injuring her legs in the race. He started to jump up and tell her to take off those shoes, but he held himself back.

The instant she sank into the pew beside him, he heard a whoosh of breath from her lungs. "These shoes are killing me," she said as she kicked them off.

A sense of relief flooded Max. For a brief moment, he'd wondered if she was real. Now he knew that she was human.

"You really shouldn't wear shoes like that after what happened to you yesterday," he advised.

The instant he said those words, he wanted to kick himself. He sounded like his mother.

But she didn't seem upset by his warning. "I know, but they're the only shoes I own that go with this dress."

Max swallowed hard. "You look very nice, Patty."

Nice? That was hardly the word for how she looked. Try breathtakingly gorgeous. Or heartstoppingly stunning.

She smiled back at him, showing her straight, white teeth. "Thank you, Max. You look nice, too."

His ears rang. This must have been what the guys used to talk about back in high school and college when they tried to describe that gut-wrenching sensation they felt around certain women. He never fully understood until now, since he'd always been behind a book.

Sure, women had eyed him appreciatively, but he always shut them out in the past. There were too many other things to do to get distracted by women. And now, all he wanted was to sit and gawk at a woman he'd just met yesterday.

The sermon was the best Max had ever heard. When the church services ended, Patty stood up, turned, and looked down at him. His insides went weak, but he managed a smile.

"Over so soon?" he asked, trying hard to sound light-hearted.

Patty nodded. "He's great, isn't he? His sermons always really make me think."

Max let out the breath he'd been holding ever since Patty had stood. Then, he managed to right himself on legs that were ready to give out at any moment. He hoped Patty wouldn't notice.

"You okay, Max?" she asked with concern.

So much for her not noticing. "Sure, I'm fine. Legs went to sleep, that's all."

"I know just the thing to wake them up," Patty said as she casually took his hand and led him to the front of the church where a group of people had gathered.

"Hi, Patty," a woman about Patty's age called.

"C'mon," Patty whispered to Max, "there are a few people I'd like you to meet."

Max stood there and nodded toward people named Denise, Bethany, and Amy, and soon several men joined them, among them the pastor. They all acted like he was one of the group, joking around and reminding him of the picnic at the Hadaways' house later on.

Finally, Gertie came over and nudged Max and Patty. "Y'all need to go home and change. Don't want you to ruin your Sunday-go-to-meetin' clothes."

Max chuckled. Gertie was quite a character, someone who was obviously a force to take seriously. No one would be able to guess that about her, though, unless she opened her mouth. The woman was small, thin, and was probably once very pretty. She wore the same shade of lipstick his grandmother had once worn: a deep red that commanded attention. She lit up the group when she smiled and made wisecracks. Max really enjoyed being around her.

"Gertie's something else, isn't she?" Patty said as they walked to the parking lot together.

"She's something else, all right," he agreed. "But I'm not sure what."

Patty looked stricken. "Gertie's the most wonderful—"

Max chuckled and cut her off. "I didn't say she wasn't wonderful. I agree with you. It's just that there's more than meets the eye to Gertie."

Patty studied him for a minute, as if she needed to make sure they were on the same page. Then she nodded. "Yes, there's much more to Gertie than anyone would guess by looking at her."

They agreed to ride together, and Max said he'd pick Patty up at her house in an hour. "That'll give me time to fix something," she said. "I hate to go empty-handed."

"What do I need to bring?" Max wondered out loud.

"Just yourself," Patty informed him. "The first time you're a guest. After that, you bring food."

Max loved what he saw when he picked her up. She wore blue jeans and a simple light blue T-shirt that had her shop logo on the pocket. Her hair was pulled up in a ponytail. No ribbons, no bows, and no jewelry. And she didn't need them. She looked as good as ever.

When they arrived at the Hadaways' house, a little boy greeted them at the door. Max bent over, grinning at the imp, and said, "You must be Jonathan."

The child nodded and replied, "And you must be the new doctor in town."

Before Max had a chance to set Jonathan straight, the little boy had taken him by the hand and pulled him around the house, into the back yard where several men were clustered, discussing whether to set up horseshoes or volleyball.

"I like volleyball," Jonathan said.

David glanced down at his nephew and up at everyone else who were already nodding. He chuckled. "Okay, volleyball it is."

Max found himself in the middle of a heated game when he glanced over and saw Patty watching him from the sidelines, a conspiratorial smirk on her face. What was going on? Before he had a chance to figure it out, Jonathan called his name just in time for him to see the volleyball headed his way. He spiked it over the net for the game point.

As soon as the game was over, Jonathan grabbed Max's hand and pulled him over to the picnic table, where he announced, "Dr. Max is the most fun grownup in the whole world."

Max glanced around at the other adults, who were all looking at him, waiting for him to say something. He tousled Jonathan's hair and said, "All grownups can be fun when they relax."

Patty folded her arms over her chest and looked down smiling, as if she didn't want him to see her. He needed to ask her if he needed to be let in on something.

Jonathan grinned up at him and smiled. "But not like you."

Denise stepped sideways toward him, cupped her hand beside her mouth, and whispered, "Jonathan likes you, Max."

"Good, I like him, too," he replied.

"No," she said, "I don't think you understand. He *really* likes you. We've all had our turn being his favorite grownup. And now look at us. This group could be renamed 'The Jonathan Hadaway Fan Club.' It means you're special."

Max heard Gertie's voice as she came up from behind, cackling. "You know what this means, right, Max?"

He spun around on his heel to face Gertie. "It means I'm honored."

She flicked her hand from the wrist and shook her head. "No, not that."

"Well?" he asked. "What, exactly does it mean?"

"It means," she answered, looking at him and speaking slowly, "that you have no choice but to move to Clearview and hang your shingle somewhere in town."

Chapter Six

Max felt his chest constrict. When he dared sneak a peek at Patty, he noticed how she was looking down at the ground and shuffling her feet. She didn't know what to say.

For that matter, neither did he. Gertie continued to stare at him, clearly waiting for a response. She was serious.

"Well, I—"

Gertie narrowed her eyes and interrupted him. "You don't have to give us an answer yet. Think about it for a day or two, then let us know."

Max opened his mouth to argue, but then thought better of it. He knew it was no use going up against the formidable force of Gertie Chalmers. She'd get what she wanted.

And what was so bad with that, he thought. This town was an incredible place, filled with quaint stores, a laid-back atmosphere, and friendly people. Quite the opposite of his home, where he'd had to live practically all his life for people to accept him.

He inhaled and let his breath out in a whoosh as he nodded. "Okay, I'll think about it." Patty's head jerked up as she threw him a startled expression. He'd surprised her by not continuing to argue. Was it possible that he might actually consider moving to Clearview? *Nah. He wouldn't. Would he?*

Before Patty had a chance to do too much more thinking, Gertie grabbed her by the arm. "C'mon, girl, you gotta go inside and help us get the grub on the table. Can't wait all day for a girl to quit daydreaming."

Patty glanced around to see if anyone else had noticed her staring off into space and was relieved to see that everyone else was preoccupied.

The back door slapped shut behind her as she entered the huge country kitchen that used to be Gertie's workshop. Now, David Hadaway was busy at the butcher block counter, chopping vegetables.

Bethany was pulling something out of the top of the double oven on the wall. The aroma was titillating, teasing Patty's nostrils. She'd never been here when there wasn't something wonderful coming out of that oven.

Denise and Amy were discussing how to arrange the desserts.

"You just want to sneak some cake onto your dinner plate," Bethany said as she came between Denise and Amy.

Denise giggled and backed away. "Okay, so you're on to me. Have it your way, Amy. You're probably right, anyway. We have to set a good example for Jonathan and Emily."

Bethany rolled her eyes, then winked at Patty and Amy before turning back to Denise. "You're so thoughtful, Denise, always thinking of the children."

"Yeah, that's me, all right." Denise turned to Patty and grinned. "C'mon, Patty. Grab that basket of rolls by the door and help me get the table set outside."

Patty wasn't much use in the kitchen, but she was good at following orders.

As Patty walked outside, she noticed how all the men turned and looked over at her. Jonathan was the only one brave enough to say something.

"You sure do look pretty today, Patty," he hollered.

She actually felt her face get hot. For the first time in her life, Patty knew she was blushing. Growing up with brothers didn't give her the opportunity to think enough about herself to do what seemed natural to most girls.

Max chuckled and added, "She sure does, doesn't she?"

Denise nudged Patty. "Can you believe those guys?

They act like they've never seen pretty women before." She put down the plates she was carrying and called out to her husband. "Hey, Andrew, can you give us a hand with the food? There's a ton of it in the kitchen that needs to be carried out."

Without having to be asked, all the other men followed Denise and Andrew inside, Jonathan happily running along behind them. He was put in charge of the napkins and condiments.

Once everything was on the table outside, David said the blessing before they all grabbed a plate. Patty jumped when Max came up behind her and touched her shoulder.

He tilted his head toward a small tree. "Would you like to spread our blanket over there? I'd like to talk to you for a few minutes."

Patty looked around and saw Denise mouthing "go ahead" from across the table. She turned back and nodded. "Uh, sure."

Max put his plate back on the table, picked up the blanket Patty had brought, and spread it beneath the tree. Then he joined her and filled his plate to capacity.

"Hungry?" Patty asked as she stifled a smile.

"Yeah, I guess I am." He looked down at her plate and raised his eyebrows. "You're not exactly eating like a bird, either."

Patty felt her insides grow warm. She'd never been a picky eater, and she'd always consumed more than all the other girls. But she was an athlete, and burned off most of what she ate.

"I love to eat," she said simply, taking the chance that he wouldn't approve. But too bad if he didn't, because that's the way she was.

"That's one of the things I like about you." He looked down at her for a long moment before she turned away. She didn't want anyone to notice how she felt, and Denise seemed to be watching her like a hawk. This was one time she wished she could be completely alone with Max. It felt awkward to have all eyes fixed on her, waiting for either her or Max to make a move. Apparently, they'd discussed their plans for her and the man they wanted to move his medical practice to Clearview. From the looks of things, they were even starting to do a little mental matchmaking.

If Patty and Max thought they might have a few moments alone to talk, they were sadly mistaken. Jonathan was right on their heels.

"I wanna sit by Dr. Max," he argued when David had tried to entice him to sit with Emily. "Emily's too messy."

They'd no sooner sat down on the blanket when something began to beep. Max slapped at his belt, glanced down, and mumbled under his breath.

"What's that noise?" Jonathan asked.

"My beeper," Max replied. "Looks like I need to make a quick call. My cell phone's in the car. Be right back." He jumped up and hightailed it around to the front of the house to his car.

The instant he left the back yard, everyone turned to see Patty's reaction. She shrugged and stuffed a bite of her roll into her mouth. Since she had no idea what was going on, she had no comment.

Max was gone for a mere five minutes before Patty spotted him walking slowly around the side of the house. He paused for a moment, until he saw her staring at him. She looked down. He didn't need to know she'd been staring a hole through the fence, waiting for him to return.

He let out a long sigh and shook his head. "My vacation's been cut short. One of my patients *needs* me."

The emphasis he'd put on the word caused her to wonder what he'd meant. He certainly didn't sound happy about having to leave Clearview.

"Aw, Max, you don't have to leave now, do you?" Denise moaned.

Max shrugged. "Afraid so. My cousin was supposed to be on call this weekend, but the patient won't even consider going to him. Says he's too young and inexperienced."

Was that disdain she heard in Max's voice? Patty wondered what kind of doctor would have this attitude toward his patients. Certainly not someone she'd want to see. This was a side to him that didn't look good.

"Would you like me to take you home before I head back?" he asked.

"No, that's okay," Patty replied. "I can get a ride from someone here."

"But I wanted a ride in that honey of a car of yours, Max," Gertie said, sounding like a disappointed child.

"Maybe some other time," Max replied as he reached over and hugged Gertie.

She shook her finger at him. "You better come back to Clearview, young man."

He chuckled, but Patty could tell his heart wasn't in it. He looked positively sullen. "Don't worry. I'll be back as soon as possible. Maybe even later on in the week."

"I'm taking that as a promise," Gertie said as she backed away. She looked at Patty. "You better give him a reason to want to come back."

He'd only been gone for a few minutes before Amy gestured to Patty to join the rest of the group. Patty reluctantly stood up, tugged at the blanket, and crossed the yard.

"He won't be gone long, ya know," Gertie said after several minutes of silence.

"That's okay," Patty said. "I'm fine."

"No, you're not." Gertie was always direct, and she wouldn't allow anyone to try to pull something over on her. "You're hurt. I can see it in your eyes." She shook her head. "I would be, too. In fact, I'd be spittin' mad."

Denise whistled. "One thing you don't wanna see is when Gertie gets mad. Whoo-boy."

Everyone laughed. Patty had heard tales of when Gertie had ripped into Bethany and Denise when they were younger.

David chimed in with stories he'd heard about Gertie's wrath. Naturally, she denied everything, but that only made everyone laugh. Bethany giggled for a while before adding a few tales of her own.

Then, Jonathan piped in, "You should have seen Grandma Gertie when I shook up the bottle of soda pop. I thought she'd never stop yelling."

"Get outta here," Gertie said. "I never fussed at you. I just told you I didn't like what you were teaching Emily."

Jonathan snorted. "Yeah, right."

Everyone had gotten back into the spirit of having fun, but Patty felt miserable. Just when she thought she'd met a man who wasn't intimidated by her, things went up in smoke. And she'd discovered that Dr. Max Dillard wasn't as wonderful as he'd seemed.

"Need a ride home?" Denise asked from behind, coming up on the right.

Amy was quickly on her other side, putting her arm around Patty's shoulders. "We're here for you, Patty. But I have a feeling he will be back."

"I don't want to count on anything," Patty said as she held herself rigid to keep from shaking. "Besides, it's better that he leave now than later."

She watched as Amy and Denise exchanged a glance behind her. It wasn't a look of pity; it was more like *what-do-we-do-now*.

"Everyone has to pitch in for clean-up," Gertie announced. "C'mon, Jonathan, let's show these slow people how it's done."

The back yard was cleared of all signs of the picnic, and the dishes were washed within an hour. Then, it was time to go home.

"Let me take you home," Amy said. She turned to her new husband, Zach, and nodded. "Why don't you get a ride from my brother and Denise?"

"Sure," Zach said, concern etched on his face. Patty had always liked Zach because he'd treated her like an equal in the car business. "Let me know if there's anything I can do."

On the way to Patty's house, Amy chatted nonstop, telling Patty all about the pretty wallpaper she and Zach had been looking at. "And I even picked one for the nursery."

"The nursery?" Patty's head snapped around. "You're gonna have a baby?" Her eyes darted to Amy's abdomen.

Amy laughed. "No, not yet, anyway. I'd like to soon, though, before it's too late."

"Oh, it's far from being too late," Patty said. "You're still pretty young. You can wait a few years."

"Not if Zach has his way. He wants a houseful of kids." Amy laughed. "And I'm sure my dad would love to have grandchildren to spoil, now that I've finally grown up."

"Yes," Patty agreed. "I'm sure he would." She'd met Amy's and Andrew's dad, and he would definitely spoil his grandchildren. And since Denise and Andrew wanted to wait a little longer and limit their family to two kids, she also knew that the pressure would be on Amy and Zach to get started soon.

When she got inside, Patty waved to Amy and closed the door. Now she was left with her own private thoughts—without interruptions from well-meaning friends.

What had happened with Max during the picnic was what she'd feared most. It validated what she'd thought in the first place: that a long distance relationship was doomed from the beginning. She needed to forget Max Dillard existed.

But could she?

Okay, I can do this, she told herself. *All I have to do is immerse myself in my work and when I'm finished, surround myself with friends.* Not too hard in Clearview.

Patty did a quick clean-up of her house, then settled down with a book. Reading before bed helped get her mind off herself and put her right to sleep.

The instant Max walked into his office, he saw what the problem was. Mr. Peterson, an elderly man who'd been a patient of his grandfather's, was refusing medical treatment by Stan because he was "such a young whipper-snapper."

Max could relate, and he felt for Stan. The exact same thing had happened to him when he'd first started in the family practice.

"Okay, Mr. Peterson, what's the problem?" Max asked, working hard to keep his exasperation from coming across.

The old man rubbed his neck and shook his head. "Can't sleep."

Max gritted his teeth. "You can't sleep?" Hardly an emergency.

"No." Mr. Peterson stretched his arms out in front of him and yawned. "Would you hurry it up, Doc? I'm missing my favorite game show. Just give me some pills, and I'll be on my way."

"Look, Mr. Peterson," Max said as calmly as he could. "Dr. Stan Dillard could have given you some pills. We need to find the root of your problem so you can get the quality rest you need."

As Max stood back, he studied Mr. Peterson. He certainly didn't look overly tired.

Mr. Peterson growled. "I know what I want, and I want pills."

"Sorry," Max said as he backed up to lean against the counter. "I won't take the risk of giving you some-thing that might compound the problem."

"Then I'll just take my business elsewhere." Mr. Peterson hopped down off the examining table and headed for the door. "You should be ashamed of yourself, young man. I've been coming here, to this office, ever since I can remember. Your grandfather always took care of me."

Max nodded. He remembered something his grandfather had told him before he retired. Some of the patients would try to bully him, but he needed to stand behind what he knew was right. And giving in to Mr. Peterson was definitely not the right thing to do.

The rest of the morning was light, since he hadn't scheduled any appointments. He still had most of his vacation coming to him, but he wasn't sure what to do. One thing he could do was to continue on his trip along the country roads, but that wasn't what he really wanted. His strongest desire was to rush right back to Clearview and see Patty again.

Her image popped into his mind, sending all sorts of emotions flooding through him. Patty was a unique woman, unlike anyone he'd ever met before. She was strong, smart, beautiful, and full of life. She was opinionated and spunky, something that made him smile every time he thought of her.

He had to see her again. Max knew he was playing with fire by going back to Clearview, but this time desire overtook reason. Patty O'Neill was worth losing his mind over.

"Hey, Max," Stan said as they headed out the door for lunch. "Sorry about Mr. Peterson. He refused to tell me what his problem was. I never would have called you back if I'd known."

Max laid a hand on Stan's shoulder. "Don't worry about it, Stan. Mr. Peterson has always been difficult to treat. Maybe it would be better if he found another doctor."

Stan slowly nodded. "I just hate to be the cause of losing a patient."

"You're not. In fact, I remember Mr. Peterson doing the exact same thing to me when I first started here. He's a bully, but he'll eventually come around. You'll see him again."

With a snicker, Stan said, "Can't wait."

"I'm going home to do a few things before I leave again," Max told his cousin. "As tempting as it is to not bring my beeper, I won't do that to you. Just make sure it's a true emergency before you call next time, okay?" He patted Stan on the back to let him know he wasn't angry.

"Sure thing, Max. Get some rest, okay?" Stan frowned, then looked at Max. "By the way, how'd you do in the race?"

Max shrugged. "Came in third."

"Third?" Stan shook his head. "I know how hard you've been training. What happened? Get distracted?"

"Something like that," Max said, not wanting to explain what was going on in his mind. Even if he knew, he didn't want to share his thoughts or feelings.

"You do need a break," Stan told him. "I'll talk to your dad before I call again. Maybe he can handle things like this. If I'd known Mr. Peterson was bluffing, I would have sent him to your dad in the first place." He looked away then back at Max. "You don't think there really is something wrong with him, do you?"

"Nah," Max replied. "But if you're worried, why don't we swing by his apartment before we eat lunch?"

Mr. Peterson lived in a high-rise retirement village not too far from the office. Max had dropped in on patients there many times, and it always delighted them.

"Sure," Stan said. "Maybe he'll start looking at me differently if I do that."

"Don't count on it."

They walked the three blocks to the retirement village, where the doorman admitted them. "G'mornin', Doc," the guard said as he nodded.

"Hi, Jack. Mr. Peterson in?"

"Yes, sir, he came right back from your office and went up in the elevator. Said he was gonna watch TV."

Max and Stan exchanged a glance. "He won't like us interrupting his favorite show, but that's too bad," Max said. "He interrupted my vacation, so I think it's okay."

When they got to Mr. Peterson's apartment, they knocked. No one answered.

"Sounds like someone's home," Stan said. The television was blaring, but there were no live voices. "Or maybe he just left the TV on."

"I don't think so," Max said. "Knock again."

Stan pounded his fist on the door, twice as loud this time. A few seconds later, they could hear the sound of the reclining chair being righted.

"I think I know what Mr. Peterson's problem is," Max said.

When the elderly gentleman came to the door, his hair was a mess and he was rubbing his eyes. They'd obviously awakened him.

"What're you doing here?" he asked Stan.

Max stepped up. "He was concerned about you, so we decided to do a house call."

Mr. Peterson grumbled and stepped back to let them in. "I was right in the middle of my show."

Max glanced at the television. "You like soaps?" Max asked.

"Never watch 'em."

Max pointed to the TV. "Looks like your game show's over, Mr. Peterson."

The old man sighed. "So it is. Maybe I dropped off for a few seconds when it was over."

Stan had picked up the TV guide on the end table and was looking at it. "This soap opera is on right after my wife's favorite series."

With a gesture toward the sofa, Max told Stan's

patient, "Have a seat, Mr. Peterson. I think I know what your problem is."

He explained to the elderly man that taking long morning and afternoon naps could interfere with regular nighttime sleep cycles. "Maybe if you get more exercise and limit naps to a half hour a day, you won't have trouble sleeping at night."

Mr. Peterson grumbled. "I've worked hard all my life. I deserve to sleep anytime I want to."

"That's true, but you came to us for treatment."

"I came to you for pills, but you wouldn't give 'em to me."

"And we're not going to, either," Stan told him. "If you really want to get quality sleep, I can help you, but only if you cooperate."

Max was proud of his cousin. In fact, it was the first time he could remember Stan ever standing up to anyone.

"Okay, okay," Mr. Peterson said. "Now if you two don't mind, I have things to do."

Stan and Max stood up and moved toward the door. Stan turned to Mr. Peterson. "If you want to find another doctor, I understand. But I think I can help you."

"I'll think about it," Mr. Peterson grumbled.

As they left, Max snickered. "You've got a patient for life."

"Oh great," Stan replied as he grinned back.

Chapter Seven

Patty was beneath the front of an old Mustang when she saw a familiar pair of shoes. She wheeled herself out from under the car and grinned.

Amy laughed. "You have grease all over your face, Patty."

Patty shrugged. "Some women wear foundation. I wear grease. What's up?"

"Phone call." Amy remained standing there, not budging.

"Tell whoever it is I'll call back." Patty didn't understand why Amy hadn't already done that; she usually did.

"It's Max."

"Oh." Patty hesitated for a moment as she tried to decide what to do. Most of the time she didn't struggle with decisions like this, but most of the time her emotions weren't on the edge of her skin.

"Want him to call back later?"

After she licked her lips, Patty shook her head no. "Just tell him I'll be a few seconds. I need to wash my hands."

Amy nodded and rushed back to the office. Patty stood up, washed her hands, and shut her eyes to bring up the image of the man who'd invaded her thoughts and dreams. The only time she could clear her mind of him was when she was working on cars.

"Patty?" Max said when she finally picked up the phone. "I was wondering if you'd like to see me tomorrow night."

"I thought you had an emergency back home." *Where was he?*

She heard Max let out a long sigh. "False alarm. My cousin's handling all the emergencies for the next two weeks, and I'd like to see you again."

Patty had no idea what to do. She'd never been in this situation before in her life, when her heart told her one thing while her mind was telling her another.

"Okay, Max, but I'll be working late. I have more cars lined up than you can imagine."

"Need help?" He actually sounded sincere.

"Well . . ."

"I really want to help, Patty," he begged.

"What time can you be here?" She had several cars that needed their oil changed and lights serviced. If he wanted to lend a hand, she knew now was time to accept it. Zach was already busy with his own shop, and she didn't want to impose on his generosity any more than she had to.

"How about four tomorrow afternoon? I have a few things to wrap up before I can get out of town."

"Okay," Patty said before she hung up.

Amy appeared at the door right when she got off the phone. "How's he doing?"

Patty stood and stared at the wall before looking at Amy. "He's coming back."

"Here?" Amy screeched in delight. "Back to Clearview?"

"Yes. In fact, he even offered to help me service a few cars."

Amy laughed. "That man has it bad for you, Patty."

Patty shuddered. "Really? What makes you say that?"

"The man's a doctor, Patty. He doesn't have to do anything he doesn't want to do." Her tone made it clear that she knew what she was talking about.

"Nothing is making any sense to me anymore, Amy. Just when I got used to the fact that things can't possibly work out between Max and me, he calls me and says he wants to see me."

"Don't ever give up hope, Patty."

"But the distance—"

"Yes, there is a considerable distance between where you live, but some things can be overcome."

A New Understanding 101

"I don't see how," Patty argued.

"Then stop trying and just let things happen as they will."

Patty fell silent for a moment as she thought about what Amy said. It still didn't sound logical to her, but maybe her partner was right. She'd always made things happen in the past, even when it didn't seem possible. Now, she needed to sit back and wait for someone else to handle the impossible.

Patty watched Amy walk away. She remembered when she'd first met Amy. It was so strange how they'd connected as friends, even though they were obviously from completely different worlds. It wasn't until much later, after she'd gotten to know Amy better, that she realized they were more alike than different.

While Amy had come from a protected environment, she'd never had a true friend who cared about her. Patty was in the same boat. All her friends in the past had been guys who liked to talk sports and cars. Other females rarely understood her or took the time to hear what was really on her mind and in her heart. But Amy was different. They had been able to get past their societal standings and reach a different level than either of them had gained before.

Patty was grateful to Amy and for the confidence her new friend had placed in her. And she wasn't about to let her down.

However, one thing Patty thought was that Amy

was sadly mistaken about Max. Amy was being overly romantic when she thought there was any chance for the two of them to ever get together for more than a short fling. In fact, all of Patty's friends were too hopeful in their thinking that Max might even consider moving to Clearview. Patty wasn't about to dump everything she was familiar with and move to the city, where she knew she'd be miserable. Traffic and skyscrapers made her jittery.

Patty managed to get back to business for the remainder of the day. She finished working on several cars before she felt justified in going home.

"I'll be in early tomorrow," Amy said. "We have a six-thirty delivery of that Rolls, and I promised someone would be here."

"You don't have to do that," Patty told her.

With a shrug, Amy replied, "I don't mind. In fact, I actually enjoy driving the cars around to the back."

Patty knew Amy was telling the truth. She'd seen Amy's eyes light up when she cranked the ignition. Some people seemed to have been born with an appreciation of old cars, and Amy was one of those people.

"Okay, if that's what you want." Patty wiped her hands on the rag she kept by the sink in the garage, then tossed it onto the table that held spare parts. "Just don't feel like you have to do stuff like that, just to help me out."

Amy's expression turned from sheer joy to pained.

"Patty, you might not be used to this, but sometimes it actually makes people feel good to help you out. That's one of the things friends do for each other."

Patty instantly felt awful for what she'd said. She hung her head and hoped she could apologize sufficiently. "I'm really sorry, Amy. I don't know why I said that."

"I understand. It's hard to accept help from others when you've always been the one to do everything."

Patty hugged her friend. "Thanks. Now we both need to get home before we start blubbering all over each other."

Shaking her head, Amy smiled back. "And that's okay, too. Nothing wrong with letting a few tears fall in front of true friends."

As Patty finished cleaning up in the shop, she counted her blessings. Amy had been so patient with her when she'd acted like a total idiot about friendship. She felt like a friend-in-training every time Amy taught her something she'd never even thought of before.

After a shower and a frozen dinner, Patty crawled into bed with a car magazine. She needed to keep her mind off seeing Max tomorrow, or she feared she'd never fall asleep.

She arose before sunup and got ready for a long day at the shop. Amy would be there when she arrived, so she took her time getting ready. Even though she knew she'd get oil and grease on her clothes over the course of the day, she liked to start out clean and fresh.

Amy's eyes were still lit with excitement when Patty pulled into the parking lot. "You wouldn't believe how that car drives," she said before Patty had a chance to open her mouth.

Patty knew exactly what Amy was talking about: the Rolls Royce. "They're great cars, aren't they?"

With a nod, Amy went on. "If they didn't cost so darn much money, I'd try to talk Zach into getting one. I'm sure he'd love it."

Patty was well aware that Amy could afford a Rolls Royce, even if Zach didn't think so, but Amy was considerate of her husband's pride.

"Maybe one of these days," Patty offered, "when our business takes off."

"Yeah, maybe one of these days," Amy said dreamily.

It was nice to have things to look forward to. Patty understood. In the past, Amy had been given everything her father thought she wanted. However, Patty also knew that Amy wasn't truly happy as an adult until she'd severed the strings that made her feel bound to her father. This was something Patty had never had to worry about. She'd been supporting herself since high school. Fortunately, she had a trade she could count on to give her what she needed and much of what she wanted.

"Looking forward to seeing Max?" Amy asked.

Patty shrugged, trying hard to hide what was really going on inside her. "I guess."

"Don't get too excited," Amy teased. "Or I just might have to tie you down." She rolled her eyes.

With a chuckle, Patty said, "I don't see any sense in getting overly excited about something that's so fleeting. Max is finishing out his vacation, then he's going back home. Maybe, if I'm lucky, I'll get to see him once a year, until he gets tired of coming to Clearview."

Amy seemed to consider what Patty had just said, nodding and staring into space for a moment. When she turned back to Patty, though, she had a strange expression on her face. "Never know about these things."

Patty shrugged as she grabbed a wrench. "I don't want to get too worked up, or I'm afraid I'll wind up disappointed and broken-hearted."

As she had more work than she could possibly get done in a day, Patty managed to stay busy all morning before she took fifteen minutes to gulp down a sandwich Amy had brought. Then she went right back to work.

"You need to take a little more time for yourself, Patty," Amy advised her. "You'll burn out if you don't."

"Yeah, that's what Max said."

"He's the doctor. He knows what he's talking about."

As Patty went back beneath the car she'd already started working on, she thought about what both Max and Amy had told her. As much as she loved car engines, she knew that too much of anything wasn't good. She'd have to loosen her schedule a little after she finished with her current commitments, which would take her at least into the next month.

A familiar masculine voice startled Patty. She almost bumped her head as she rolled herself out from beneath the car. Max was standing above her, his legs shoulder-width apart, his arms folded over his chest.

"Sorry I'm late," he said.

"You're not—" she began. But when she glanced up at the clock, she saw that it was half an hour past the time he'd agreed to be there. "I guess you are, but that's okay."

"No, it's not," he said with a contrite voice. "I hate it when I don't honor my word."

Oh, great, she thought. *He's not only the most wonderful guy I've ever met, he's the most honorable one, too.* "Then I forgive you," she said with a shaky smile. Max studied Patty as she remained lying on the dolly. How could a woman look so stunning with all that black grease on her nose?

"That's a relief. Here, let me give you a hand."

He quickly pulled her to her feet then let go. The electrical current that flowed between them was intense, and he didn't want to take a chance and get too distracted. After all, he'd offered to help her do a little service work on some cars so she could justify spending time with him while he was in Clearview.

"Whaddya want me to start on first?" he asked.

She looked him over as he stood before her. "Don't you want to change first?"

He held his hands out and looked down at himself. "This is all I've got."

Pointing to the wall, she said, "Grab a pair of coveralls off the hook. There's a restroom over behind the office. You can change there."

Max nodded and did as he was told. Patty was very explicit in her orders, and he didn't mind following them. For once, someone else was in control, which gave him some relief.

When he came out, she was still standing beside the car she'd been working on. "Not a bad fit, huh?"

He shook his head. "No, in fact, they fit perfectly."

"Okay," she said as she pushed past him and headed toward the other side of the garage. "I've already got the first car ready for the oil change. That's all you have to do on this one. I've checked it over for everything else. When you're done here, just back it out and pull the green Chevy behind the yellow line."

Something else he loved about Patty was that she was so organized and competent. She didn't depend on anyone for any kind of support.

He saluted her and did as he was told. Looking over his shoulder, he saw that she was staring at him, worry lines etched on her forehead. What was that all about?

*   *   *

Patty felt like kicking herself in the backside. She'd been told she was bossy, yet she forgot to tone it down with Max. What would he think? She didn't want to scare him away—not yet, anyway.

"Uh, Max," she said as she edged toward him. "I'm sorry about how I come across sometimes. I tend to be a little, er . . . uh . . ."

"In control?" he asked with a smile. "Don't worry about it. I'm used to it, being around doctors all day."

Patty let out a sigh of relief. He acted like he really meant what he said. "Thanks."

She turned around to finish her work on the car she'd started, leaving Max to do what she'd assigned . . . no, ordered him to do. And for some reason she'd probably never understand, he didn't get bent out of shape over her tone.

Max certainly seemed perfectly happy. In fact, he was actually whistling. The men she'd worked with in the past had been sullen after she'd bossed them around. They were all capable mechanics, and they resented her knowing more than they knew about classic cars.

Max, on the other hand, actually listened to her, and when he asked her a question, he did exactly what she recommended. Then he complimented her on how well she knew her stuff.

As soon as she was finished with her car, Patty went to the sink and scrubbed her fingernails with the brush she kept there for that purpose. Max completed the lube he was working on then joined her.

"Not bad for just a couple of hours, huh?" he asked, glancing over his shoulder at the line of cars he'd worked on.

"No, not bad," she agreed. "In fact, you're faster and more thorough than most mechanics I've worked with in the past. Where'd you learn your way around a car?"

Max shrugged. "While all the other doctors' kids were getting brand new sports cars from their parents, my dad told me to find a way to earn my own. All I could afford was what most of my friends considered junk." He chuckled. "The joke was on them when I sold my car and made a few bucks, while they all took a beating when they tried to trade their cars in for the newest models."

"What do you drive now, besides that Cadillac?" Patty asked.

"That's all I have now," he replied. "Cars have never been my hot button, so when I found that beauty, I got rid of my Honda that had seen better days. Can you believe I put almost two hundred thousand miles on it?"

"Absolutely," Patty said. "When you keep the oil changed and do regular maintenance on a car, it can run for a long time."

"And since I had to learn to take care of cars myself,

I never had to take it to a shop until it needed major repairs."

Patty admired Max for this. He was a doctor and the son of a doctor, which meant he could probably have anything he wanted.

"Do you live in a house?" she asked.

"I have a condo. Much simpler to maintain." Max stopped for a minute. "But you don't seem to have a problem taking care of a house. How do you do so much and look like you do?"

Patty scrunched her nose. "What do you mean by that?"

Max held his hands out. "I don't know. Everything seems to come so easy to you. You have this successful business, you live in a nice house that's well taken care of, you're in great shape, and you always seem to be surrounded by friends. People all like you for who you are, not what you do."

"I'm not so sure about that," Patty countered. "And I haven't always been surrounded by friends. In fact, before I met Amy, I hardly had any girlfriends at all. Since I work on cars, most of my acquaintances are guys."

Max's expression changed as he glanced away. She had no idea what he was thinking, but something she'd said had definitely altered the mood.

Did he dare hope that Patty would have time for him in her life? Max wondered to himself. She'd just admitted that she knew a lot of men. And looking like she did, as nice as she was, he had no doubt they all wanted to take the relationship beyond friendship.

Max decided right then and there to test the waters carefully before making any life-altering decisions. He'd been doing some heavy thinking after being called back home. When what Gertie had proposed started making sense, Max began to worry. Yes, he wanted to think about moving to Clearview. But he had to hold back and see if it was in his best interest.

"Where would you like to have dinner?" he asked. "Burger Barn?"

She belted out a deep laugh. "No, I don't think so. The thought of grease after all this work today doesn't appeal to me in the least."

"Are there any decent restaurants around here?"

"There's one on the other side of town, but I'm not in the mood for seafood. How do you feel about taking a drive to Plattsville?"

"How far is that?"

"About twenty minutes," Patty replied, glancing down at her watch. "There's a really nice restaurant there called the Pine Room, and I'm in the mood for a steak. How 'bout you?"

He hesitated. Max was tired of driving, but if Patty wanted to go somewhere twenty minutes away, he'd do it. Besides, a steak sounded good.

"Okay," he said. "That sounds fine."

She offered a brisk nod. "Good. I'll drive." Then

she softened for a moment and offered a shaky smile. "Sorry, I'm doing it again. Do you mind if I drive?"

Max chuckled. "No, I don't mind at all. In fact, I prefer it."

Chapter Eight

"This is the life," Max said after a long sigh.

Patty glanced over and saw the contented grin on Max's face as he clasped his fingers behind his head. He really did look relaxed and in good spirits.

"We're only going to the Pine Room. It's good, but I don't want you to be disappointed."

He turned and looked at her, still smiling. "I don't care where we're going. My vacation has started again, and I'm being driven on a date by the most beautiful auto mechanic this side of the Mississippi."

Patty tightened her grip on the steering wheel as the heat rushed to her cheeks. She should know better than to take his compliment to heart.

But then his stare did her in. "What?" she said as she continued watching the road ahead.

113

"You don't know, do you?"

She cast a quick glance in his direction, then refocused on the road. "Don't know what?"

"How beautiful you are."

Max reached out and touched her hair. She wanted to grab hold of his hand, but she didn't dare.

"I . . . uh, well . . ." What could she say to that?

"Patty, you're sweet, smart, pretty, and fun to be with. In fact, you're the reason I came back."

As Max spoke, Patty's heart rate rose to a whole new level. Did she dare to believe him? And so what if she did? The whole thing would be over soon, since he had to get back home when his two-week vacation was over.

Max pulled his hand back and laughed out loud. "I can't believe this."

"Can't believe what?"

"That you're not used to people telling you how wonderful you are."

She shrugged, trying to act like his words weren't affecting her, but she knew she wasn't fooling anyone. "I just don't know what to say, that's all."

"Patty," Max said softly, "you don't have to say anything. I'm telling you what I think. I'd like to get to know you better."

She swallowed hard. No way could she deny that she wanted to get to know him too, but what good would that do?

Fortunately, they'd reached the edge of Plattsville.

"I hope you like the Pine Room. It's almost everyone's favorite place to go for special occasions."

"This is a very special occasion, and I'm glad we're going there."

Each time Max spoke to her, Patty felt her hopes rise. But what could she hope for, other than to spend two glorious weeks with the only man who'd held her interest over anything besides a carburetor?

The waiter recommended the rib eye special. Max nodded and motioned to Patty. "How's that sound to you?"

She nodded to the waiter. "Sounds good to me."

"Me, too," Max said before turning his full attention to her. "Anything would sound good to me right now, even a peanut butter and jelly sandwich." He reached out across the table and took her hand. "Being with you feels like heaven on earth."

Patty blinked as she stared at Max. No man had ever said such sweet words to her, so she wasn't sure if she was dreaming.

"I–I don't know what to say," she stuttered.

"You don't have to say anything. Just enjoy the moment."

The entire evening was like a fairy tale come alive for Patty. Now she knew what was meant by the expression "swept off her feet." She wanted to see more of Max, but she also feared losing her heart to someone who could never give his. The geographical distance between them was too great.

Amy had plenty of advice for her the next morning. "Just enjoy being with him. If it's meant to be, things will work out."

"Easy for you to say." Patty hung her head and stared at the coveralls that hung on the hook. She'd already been at the shop for fifteen minutes and hadn't put them on yet.

"I remember what it felt like, back when I saw Zach at the car shows. And when I thought there was no chance things would ever work out between us because I wasn't the type of woman he usually dated, I gave up hope. I was worried what my dad would think, too. And now look."

Amy held out her hand and showed off the small, sparkling diamond engagement ring and wedding ring set she proudly wore. It was a fraction of the size of what her father probably wanted her to have, but it was what Zach could afford.

"Fat chance of anything like that ever happening to me," Patty said. "No man wants to fall in love with a grease monkey."

With a soft giggle, Amy shook her head. "You're such a cute grease monkey, I don't see how any man could resist. Besides, I'm sure you'll throw in an occasional free oil change to go with the deal."

Patty rolled her eyes and turned around. She loved

girl talk and kidding around with Amy, who seemed to understand her better than anyone.

"See you at lunch. I brought some chicken salad and stuck it in the fridge," Amy called after her as she made her way back to the shop.

One of the things they'd done when designing the office was to install a fully equipped kitchen. Patty knew there would be days when she wouldn't have time to go out for lunch. And Amy didn't seem to mind cooking and bringing food to work. Patty knew that Amy had been brought up in a home with a full-time cook, chauffeur, and maids, so every domestic thing she'd learned had been since she'd been out on her own. Patty admired Amy for forcing herself to learn skills as an adult that most people learned growing up.

Patty had already gotten involved in rebuilding the engine of an old Thunderbird when she heard Max's and Amy's voices in the shop. She stopped what she was doing, put down her wrench, and came around from behind the car to see what was going on. She saw the conspiratorial look on their faces.

"What're you two up to?" she asked.

Max came toward her, causing her pulse to quicken. But he stopped before he was close enough to touch her.

"We're making big plans," Amy said. "And I'll leave the two of you alone and get back to the office." She turned and was gone in a flash.

As soon as Amy was out of sight, Patty turned to Max. "Okay, what gives?"

"I've come to take you away from all this," he said softly. "That is, after I do a few oil changes and lubes."

Patty crinkled her nose and looked at him, her head tilted. "Are you sure you wanna do that? This isn't much of a vacation for you."

He shrugged. "Can't think of anything else I'd rather do at the moment."

"Well," she said as she moved toward the work table and picked up some tools he'd need. "You know the routine. Grab some coveralls and have at it." Gesturing toward the right side of the garage, she added, "All the cars in that line-up need oil changes and a quick check of the vital parts."

"Sounds like medical work to me. In fact, you're just like me. A steady stream of patients all lined up, no end to your day in sight."

Patty snorted. "I guess you can call me Dr. O'Neill if you want. I have to finish this operation, then do a major transplant on that old Ford back there." She pointed to the car right behind the Thunderbird.

"See? I was right." Max turned and headed toward the pegs where Patty hung clean coveralls.

They worked in silence for more than an hour. Patty allowed herself a peek at Max every few minutes, and she found him deeply engrossed in his work. Never in her wildest dreams could she have imagined anything like this happening to her. Max was a doctor, for heaven's sake. He had no reason to do all this dirty work.

At the moment, Max felt like things were starting to make sense. There was something about working on cars that gave him a strong sense of accomplishment. Perhaps it was the fact that they didn't have minds of their own and they never talked back.

Patty was obviously good at what she did. She had more business than he'd ever seen in an auto shop, and this was a highly specialized one at that. From the counties and states listed on the auto tags, he knew she'd developed a reputation all over for quality work.

A sense of pride flooded Max. He was participating in something worthwhile—preserving a piece of history—each time he serviced one of these automobiles.

Clearview was a town that affected him, mind, body, and soul, in a unique way. Instead of being filled with high rises, high incomes, and high-tech everything, the town emanated a down-home feel. People cared about each other. They had social gatherings where all they did was talk, laugh, and play backyard games.

Maybe he was nuts, but he wanted that for himself. He wanted to feel like he truly belonged and would be missed if he ever left. His desire was to fit in, simply because he was himself and not because he generated a certain amount of income or expertise in his field of medicine.

Gertie had begun planting the seeds of desire for him to move here. But he couldn't just up and leave his family practice. Could he?

No, that wouldn't happen. Too many commitments. Too many irons in the fire. Too many people depending on him.

Max was exhausted just thinking about it. He didn't have any sort of social life, and his professional life was centered around a select few patients who paid him well to cater to their whims. Sure, he'd developed a reputation for being the best at diagnosing problems and treating them, but he wanted more than that. He wanted to really get to know his patients, to care about their families, and to be honest, he wanted them to like him as a person, too.

"Ready for lunch?" Amy called from the door of the shop, interrupting his thoughts.

"Lunch?" Max said as he glanced at the clock on the wall. It was already twelve-thirty. Where had time gone?

Patty tossed her tools onto the table and moved over to the sink. She looked over her shoulder and winked.

"Amy's a great cook, and she brought lunch."

"Uh, that's okay," Max said. He hadn't considered the fact that he might be intruding if he just showed up today. All he cared about was seeing Patty, and he was willing to work all day to do that. "I can go out."

"Don't be silly," Amy told him. "Gertie told me you might show up, so I made plenty of chicken salad. C'mon."

She turned and headed down the hall that connected the office, kitchen, and waiting area to the shop. He turned to Patty. "You sure it's okay?"

Patty raised her eyebrows and nodded. "We don't say anything we don't mean around here."

That was another thing Max loved about this place. People didn't play games in their relationships. They said what they meant and meant what they said. Novel concept.

"This is the most delicious chicken salad I've ever tasted," Max said. He meant it, too.

Amy blushed. "Thanks, Max. Gertie gave me the recipe."

Patty took another bite of her cracker and pointed to the wall in the kitchen, where a shelf was filled with cookbooks. "Gertie sends everyone off with recipes. It's one of the rites of passage to adulthood."

Max blinked. "There must be a dozen books up there."

"All of them were filled by things Gertie has cooked in her own kitchen, where the Hadaways now live."

He stood up, crossed the room, and pulled out one of the cookbooks. The title, *Recipes From Members of New Hope Community Church*, was simple and to the point.

"Did everyone in the church contribute?" he asked as he flipped through the pages.

Patty nodded. "Yeah, but almost everyone learned to cook things that Gertie made first. She hands out recipes like she's afraid people might starve to death if she didn't."

All the cookbooks were collections from various groups in Clearview. And all of them were filled with down-home recipes that were lovingly written by people in this town.

A pang of desire to be a part of Clearview shot through Max. He was quickly falling in love with this place. And if he wanted to be honest with himself, he had to admit his feelings for Patty were edging beyond friendship as well.

Patty wasn't the least bit pretentious. She was smart, but had no desire to impress anyone with what she knew.

He replaced the cookbook he'd been holding and sat back down with Patty and Amy. "Clearview must have the best cooks in the world."

"I think so," Amy replied.

Patty laughed, and her ponytail swished from side to side. He wanted to reach out and touch her cheek, but he held back.

"Do you cook for yourself?" Amy asked. "Or do you generally go out?"

"Sometimes I go out, sometimes my mom invites

me over—that is, if they're not entertaining one of Dad's patients."

Amy nodded her understanding. "My dad used to do a lot of entertaining, but he expected me to help him when I lived at home. My mother was so good at it, I only had to stand back and smile."

"My mom's good at it, too." Max looked at Patty, who had remained quiet during this discussion.

What could she be thinking? He saw pain in her expression, which made him want to reach out and pull her to him, to protect her and let her know how much he cared. However, he knew that making moves at the wrong time might push her further into her own thoughts and make it more difficult for him to ever understand her.

One of Patty's old insecurities was rearing its ugly head. She always felt like she didn't fit in when she was growing up, so now, when her new friends re-hashed old times, she just kept her mouth shut. After all, she had nothing to contribute. If she tried, every-one around her would realize how socially inept she was.

"How much more do you have to do today, Patty?" Amy asked.

"I still have to finish the car I'm working on now and the one right behind it. Then I've been asked to do a rush job on that VW van."

"The one with the peace sign on the back?" Amy asked.

"Yeah, that's the one. I'm amazed the thing's still running," Patty said. "It's been maintained better over the past couple of years than it was when it was new."

"People never realized how important their investments were back then, I guess," Amy said. "I love my Mustang."

Patty turned to Max and explained. "Amy secretly purchased a red Mustang convertible at one of the car shows."

"Why secretly?" Max asked.

"I didn't know what I was doing, and I didn't want anyone to laugh at me," Amy said.

This was the first time Patty had heard that explanation. She'd always thought Amy wanted to hide the fact that she had the means to purchase such an expensive car.

"You were worried about people laughing at you?" Patty asked incredulously.

Amy nodded. "Yes, I was ashamed at my lack of knowledge."

Well, that beat all, Patty thought. She never thought about anyone being ashamed besides her.

"People should never be ashamed of anything they can't control," Max said. "I used to be embarrassed about my father being a doctor."

"You were?" Patty had never heard something so outrageous in her life. "I would think you'd be proud."

Max shook his head. "He'd seen so many of my friends and their parents naked, I was almost embarrassed to look them in the eye."

Both Patty and Amy burst out laughing. "Now that's a good one," Amy said. "And I thought it was awful to have a stodgy old chauffeur take me to school when all my friends had shiny new cars they drove themselves."

As much as Patty wanted to continue the conversation, she was uncomfortable, plus she knew it was time to get back to work. "We better head on back to the shop, or we'll never be able to leave this afternoon."

"Speaking of this afternoon," Max said. "How about going somewhere for dinner and maybe a movie tonight?"

Before she had a chance to think of a reason why not, Patty nodded. "Sounds good. And don't think you have to hang around here all day, Max. You've helped out quite a bit."

"My pleasure." The sincerity of his grin let her know that he meant what he said. He really was enjoying helping her.

After Max finished all the cars that only needed oil changes and basic service work, he came up behind her and watched for a moment. She was well aware of his presence, although he didn't say a word.

The only thing that steadied her nerves when Max

was around was having her hands on a car engine. It was the only time she felt like she was in her element.

"Hey, Patty, you're good at this," Max finally said with an appreciative tone.

"Been doing it all my life."

He pulled a stool from the corner and propped one hip on it. "Most guys don't know as much about cars as you do. I'm really impressed."

Patty stopped turning the wrench and looked at him. If someone else had said those same words, she might have been offended. But with Max she wasn't, perhaps because she knew he was just being honest and not condescending.

"My dad was a mechanic before he retired, and my brothers have their own shops," she informed him. Instead of going back to the engine, she continued watching him, waiting for a response.

"Do they work on vintage cars, too?"

"No. My dad used to tinker with them on his own time, but he didn't think he could make a living at working on old cars. One of my brothers has a regular shop, and the other one only works on foreign cars."

Patty held Max's gaze before he broke the spell by being the first to look away. "I'm still in awe of what you've done here, Patty. It took two things most people don't have."

"What's that?"

"Guts and know-how."

She laughed nervously and picked up the wrench,

which kept her hands from shaking. "A lot of people know their way around cars."

"That's where the guts comes in," he said. "And I have a feeling you could probably run circles around other mechanics."

"Speaking of running," Patty said as she leaned back over the engine. "I'm going to start running again so I don't have a repeat performance of what happened at the Cross Country Run."

"Good idea. Wanna start tomorrow?"

Patty peeked at him, but he'd already turned halfway around. "Sure. We can go to the high school track and do laps."

Max had turned on the faucet and was washing his hands, using the nail brush Patty kept there. She used the opportunity to look at him without him knowing.

"What time do you want me to pick you up tonight?" Max asked as he wiped his hands on the towel.

She quickly glanced away and shrugged. "Seven-thirty all right?"

"Sounds good. I was thinking we could go to one of the new restaurants I saw on the edge of town when I drove in."

"Either that or I could cook," Patty told him.

"One of Gertie's recipes?"

"Of course. What else is there?"

"We can do that tomorrow night after we run," Max said. "But tonight I want to take you out."

As soon as Max left, Patty turned her attention back

to the car. She wanted to drop everything and run after him, but she didn't. Besides, she'd see him in a few hours.

She finished the car she was working on and started on the one behind it. Amy called the people whose cars were ready and told them they could pick them up.

"We got a lot accomplished today," Amy said. "Having an extra hand around here sure is nice."

"Yeah," Patty agreed, "but I have a feeling we won't be able to convince Max to leave his medical practice to become an auto mechanic."

"Maybe not, but we do need to think about bringing someone in for the basic stuff."

Amy's arms were folded over her chest as she maintained eye contact with Patty. Amy was right. The work load was getting to be too much, and some of the work didn't require more knowledge than any auto mechanic would have.

"We can run an ad in next Sunday's paper," Patty told her. "Why don't you call over there and see when we need to give them the information?"

With a smile, Amy said, "I already took care of that. They're just waiting for me to fax it to them."

"You called?"

"Yes. I wanted to make sure it was okay with you before I committed, though. I'm glad I didn't have to talk you into it."

Patty chuckled. "It's pretty scary when you and I start to think alike."

"It was bound to happen, with us together so much." Amy turned and headed for the office to fax the ad to the newspaper, while Patty began cleaning the shop.

After she had all the tools put away and the rags in the basket to be cleaned, Patty shed her coveralls and dropped them in with the rags. It was time to go home and get ready for her date with Max.

Her date with Max. This was something she never imagined for herself. Sure, she'd had a few dates in her past, but not with someone like Max. And definitely not with someone who looked at her like he did.

Chapter Nine

Max didn't want to say anything, but the food at Charlie's Diner was awful. Patty sat across the booth from him, eating slowly and making polite conversation. She seemed more subdued than usual.

Finally, he couldn't take it anymore. He had to find out what was bothering her. "Are you okay?"

She nodded but didn't speak at first. It seemed like she was holding something back.

"Did I say something wrong, Patty?" Max asked. Normally, he never worried about what he said because he was a straight-shooter, but now, with Patty, it mattered.

"No," she replied slowly. "It's just that I'm having a hard time choking down this food that tastes like everything came from a mix."

Max belted out a laugh. He couldn't help the booming sound he made when a flood of relief washed over him.

"I couldn't agree more," he finally managed to say between snorts.

She laid her fork on the plate and folded her hands on the table in front of her place setting. "I can't imagine them staying in business very long."

"Me, neither." Max found her politeness amusing.

"Normally, I don't have trouble eating everything on my plate, but at the risk of being kicked out of the clean plate club, I'm finished."

Max grabbed the check, stood, and reached for her hand. "Let's go grab something at the Burger Barn, where you're guaranteed satisfaction."

Patty jumped up and took his hand. Max paid the bill and led Patty to his car, where they eagerly got in to get away from the worst meal he'd ever eaten at a restaurant.

"I'm willing to bet they don't last a year," Max said as he cranked the engine.

"I put my money on them closing in two months," Patty replied. "You're probably right."

"At least the food at the Burger Barn tastes good."

Patty shifted in her seat so her body was facing Max. He felt his insides go weak.

"Clearview is due for a decent restaurant. I hate that we have to go to Plattsville to get a good meal."

"It won't be long, I'm sure," Max told her. "In fact,

I have a feeling Charlie's Diner will change hands at least once before they completely shut down."

"Really? Have you seen that happen before?"

"Lots of times. There's a restaurant on the corner near my office that went through several changes in management before they finally settled on something decent. Now it's one of my favorite places to eat."

"I hope that happens at Charlie's Diner," Patty said. She turned back to face the front, her hands in her lap.

Silence fell over them as Max drove to the Burger Barn. It wasn't an uncomfortable kind of quiet, though. In fact, he felt very relaxed and refreshed. Patty was an easy person to be around.

When they arrived in the parking lot, Max turned to Patty and said, "Wanna go inside or pick up something and take it back to your house?"

"Let's go inside," Patty said.

Max hopped out and ran around to her side right after she got out. "I was gonna get the door for you," he said sheepishly, "but I guess I was too slow."

Her lips twitched as she started to smile at him. "I guess you were."

They went inside, placed their order with the freckle-faced teenager, paid, and sat down to wait for their number to be called. Patty had started telling him about some of the cars she'd bought and sold over the years when they heard a loud groaning sound coming from the back of the dining room. When they turned around, all they saw were three small children sitting at a table, one of them in a high chair, all looking down on the floor. The oldest of the three looked scared as he said, "Mommy?"

Max quickly jumped up and ran over to see what was going on. When he glanced over his shoulder, he saw that Patty was right on his heels.

He dropped to his knees when he saw the children's mother, a young woman who appeared to be in her twenties, on her back, her eyes rolling back in her head. She was also obviously pregnant.

His medical knowledge kicked into high gear. He ran his fingers in front of her face and barked an order for Patty to call for an ambulance. Then he turned back to the woman on the floor. "Can you see my fingers?"

She moaned and tried to speak, but she couldn't. The children all sat silently, watching and waiting.

Patty did exactly what Max had ordered her to do, then went back to see if she could help. She figured that taking care of the children would be the most important thing she could do now.

Turning to the little boy, who appeared to be around four or five, she said, "Is this your mother?"

He nodded. "Is she gonna die?"

Patty's heart twisted as she realized how intense his fear was. She reached out and hugged him as she said, "No, honey, I don't think so. This man's a doctor, and he'll take very good care of her until the ambulance gets here. Can I call someone? Your father?"

The child nodded again, but he didn't say a word.

His chin was trembling as he tried hard to keep from crying.

"Do you know your phone number?" Patty asked.

The little boy shook his head.

"Your last name?"

"Smith," he said.

Patty inhaled deeply, then slowly let out her breath. Even in Clearview, there were enough Smiths to keep her on the phone for a long time looking for the right one.

"What's your father's first name?" she asked.

"Daddy," he said quickly, a flash of hope flickering across his face.

Patty glanced over at Max, who was still trying to help the woman. Her purse sat on the table beside the empty hamburger wrappers.

"Let me see if I can find some identification," Patty said as she grabbed the purse.

The little boy started crying and screaming, causing Max to glance over his shoulder. Patty dropped the purse. "What's wrong?"

His little chin was still quivering as he asked, "Are you a robber?"

"Oh, no, honey, I just need to find out how to reach someone. Is your father home right now?"

The boy shook his head. "He's at work right now, and he won't be home for two days."

"Do you know where he works?" Patty asked.

"New York," he replied.

Maybe his parents were divorced, Patty thought. And the mother was pregnant. How awful!

Her mind kicked into high gear as she knew she had to quickly decide what to do. She'd call Gertie! Gertie knew everyone in town. Maybe she'd have an idea how to get in touch with someone.

Patty pulled Max's cell phone from her back pocket and dialed Gertie's number. The elderly woman answered on the second ring.

As Patty explained the situation, Gertie listened with rapt attention. "Let me talk to the little boy," she finally said.

Patty handed the child the phone and listened to his side of the conversation. She was amazed at how much he talked to Gertie.

"Brian   Smith . . . four-and-a-half . . . Yes . . . Julie . . . Les." He nodded a few times, then handed Patty the phone. "She wants to talk to you again."

"Did you catch the names, Patty?" Gertie asked.

"Yes. I heard him say Brian, Julie, and Les."

"I asked him what his name was, and he told me Brian. When I asked him what his daddy called his mommy, he said Julie, and his mommy calls his daddy Les."

Now why hadn't Patty thought of that? "Thanks, Gertie. Do you know this family?"

"Afraid not," Gertie told her. "They must be one of the new families in town. This place is growing so fast, I feel like a stranger around here."

"I'm not sure what to do next," Patty said.

"Just watch after those children and let Max take care of the mother. She's in competent hands."

As Patty clicked off the phone, she knew that Gertie was right. Although she'd never seen Max in medical action before, she had no doubt he knew all the right things to do.

The ambulance arrived within five minutes, and Max left with them. He tossed the keys to his car to Patty and instructed her to meet him at the hospital.

Patty went to the counter and asked the teenage boy to hold onto the food. He'd witnessed the action, so he nodded and said, "No problem. Just take care of those kids."

She went back to the table where they were still sitting, not making a sound. "Why don't we go see your mommy at the hospital?" she said to Brian.

He hesitated for a moment before he slowly nodded. "You won't hurt my baby sister and little brother, will you? Mommy told me I'm supposed to take care of them."

Patty's heart melted at how brave this child was. She could only imagine what was going through his mind right now and how afraid he must be.

"I promise to take good care of all of you," she replied. "Let's go."

"Brenna's car seat is in the van," Brian told her. "Let me get Mommy's keys out of her purse, and you can get it."

It took Patty several minutes to figure out how to arrange the children, but she finally did it. Although she didn't have much experience with people this young, she went with her gut instincts, which seemed to be working for her.

They arrived at the hospital and parked in the emergency room lot. Brian held his little brother's hand while Patty carried the baby. She had maternal feelings she'd never experienced before.

As a knot formed in her chest, Patty went through the double doors with the three children. The woman at the counter looked up and nodded as she smiled at Brian. "You must be Brian Smith," she said. "I've heard some mighty nice things about you."

Patty tilted her head and looked at the receptionist. How did she know?

The woman smiled up at her and answered her question before she even asked. "Gertie Chalmers called and told me to expect you. Have a seat, and I'll get something for the children."

Within a few minutes, the woman was back with a coloring book for Brian, a plastic toy car for Joey, and a plush toy for Brenna. It looked to Patty like she'd been ready for them before they arrived.

"How's their mother?" Patty asked.

The receptionist smiled. "I think she's doing just fine, thanks to that nice doctor from out of town. He probably saved her life."

A sense of pride welled in Patty's chest. "What was wrong with her?"

"She'd gone into a diabetic coma," the receptionist replied.

"Diabetic coma?" Patty shrieked. "But she's pregnant."

"Yes, and she gave birth to a beautiful daughter. You wouldn't happen to know how to reach the father, would you?"

Shaking her head, Patty felt a sense of dread. What would she do with these children if the mother was in the hospital and they couldn't find the father?

"No idea," she said in a squeaky voice.

Patty sat in the waiting room for half an hour before Max came out to check on her. "Sorry about that, Patty," he said. "But it looks like everything's gonna be just fine. Hungry?"

"Not anymore," she said. "I found out what their names are."

Max nodded. "Yeah, so did I. The mother came to right after we arrived at the hospital. She almost didn't make it."

"Has someone contacted her husband?"

Max shook his head. "He's in New York at a banking conference, which probably means he won't be getting back to his room until late tonight. We left a message."

"What about these kids?"

With a sigh, Max raked his fingers through his hair.

"I'm not sure, I certainly can't take them since I'm staying in a hotel."

Patty had never been around children much, so she wasn't sure how competent she'd be. "I–I guess I can take them home with me, but—"

A loud rustling sound came from the automatic doors. Patty and Max both looked up. Relief flooded Patty's veins as she saw Denise storming toward them with Bethany, Amy, and Gertie on her heels. The baby relief troops.

"I got here as soon as I could," Denise said. "Gertie called Bethany, and I went around and picked 'em all up." She turned to the baby, who was holding onto the plush animal, inspecting it. "You little doll baby," Denise said as she lifted the baby from the carrier. "I could just eat you up."

"She's my baby sister," Brian informed everyone. "Her name's Brenna."

"Well, Brenna, how would you like to come home with me?" Denise was now hugging the little girl.

Brian's chin quivered as he looked at Patty. "I'm supposed to watch over her. I promised Mommy."

Denise sucked in a breath and slowly let it out. "I have an idea. Why don't we all go to my house? We can have a party."

Amy and Patty exchanged a glance. They both had to be at work early tomorrow. Gertie spoke for all of them.

"Sounds like an excellent idea. We can stay up all

night and eat cake and cookies." She was looking at Brian when she spoke.

His little face lit up. "Really?" he said with excitement, then his expression became sullen. "Mommy won't like that."

Max pulled Patty from the group. "Their mother won't be getting out of the hospital for a few days. And even if we're able to get in touch with their father, there's no way he'll be able to get here before morning."

"Then looks like we'll all be going to Denise's," Patty said. She didn't see any other solution. If it had been up to her, she would have gone home alone and let the more experienced people deal with the children. But she'd already gained Brian's confidence, and she didn't want him to be any more afraid than he was.

Max tilted his head in a nod. "Rain check on the dinner?"

"Sure," Patty replied.

"C'mon, then," Denise said as she grabbed Joey's hand with the baby in her other arm. "What're we waitin' for?"

"What about pajamas?" Brian asked.

"I have sortie old T-shirts you guys can wear. The baby's fine."

Brian glanced over his shoulder to make sure Patty was with them. She handed Max his car keys. "See you tomorrow?"

"I'll call you," Max said. "I'll be here for a little

while to make sure Mrs. Smith is doing okay, then I'll go on back to the hotel room."

He was once again amazed at the closeness of the people in this town. They didn't even know the Smith family, yet they were willing to watch after the children until the parents were able to care for them. This never would have happened back home.

When he went up to talk to Julie Smith, he explained that her children were in good hands. He talked about the slumber party and did everything he could to give her assurance.

"You have nothing to worry about."

She smiled weakly and turned away. "Did you ever get a hold of Les?" she asked in a weak voice.

"Not yet, but we have messages at the desk of his hotel and on the voicemail at the bank where he's meeting," Max said.

"He'll be so worried." Her voice cracked, and a tear trickled down her cheek. "I got gestational diabetes during my third pregnancy, and the doctor advised me to stop after Brenna. But I wanted one more child. I thought I was home free, but then I went into labor at the Burger Barn."

Max chuckled. "At least the baby's fine. Have you and your husband got a name picked out?"

She grinned at him. "No, we can't seem to decide on a name. What's your name?"

Shaking his head, he replied, "You don't want to name her after me, that's for sure. My name's Max."

"Max," she repeated. Turning to him, she said, "Thanks, Max."

"I was only doing what I was trained to do."

"Are you a medic?"

"I'm a doctor."

"You are?" Her grin widened. "Yes, I guess you are. You're an angel, Dr. Max."

He reached out and touched her face for reassurance. "Go to sleep, Mrs. Smith. Get plenty of rest because you'll need it with four children."

She nodded and closed her eyes. Max backed out of the room. He wasn't kidding when he said she'd need rest. Four children would drain the energy from anyone.

When Max finally got back to his hotel room, he flopped over on the bed. This was one of the longest days he could remember. And one of the most fulfilling. Taking care of people like Julie Smith was what he'd always wanted to do.

His medical practice had become stale. He wasn't needed for important situations where he could really make a difference. In fact, Max felt more like an order taker for pills. He wanted to do more with his training.

After turning on the television and channel surfing until he knew there wasn't anything he cared to see, he picked up the local phone directory, found Denise and Andrew's number, and dialed it. Gertie answered.

"Hi, Max," she said before he even identified himself.

"How'd you know it was me?"

"Caller I.D. You're the only one I know staying at the Clearview Hotel. What's up? You get a hold of the father?"

"No, I haven't tried, but the mother's doing fine. Tell the kids."

Gertie cupped her hand over the mouthpiece of the phone and hollered, "Hey, kids, your mom's doing fine." Then she came back to Max. "Whatcha want?"

"I was just calling to check up on all of you." He felt odd, now that he wasn't sure what he'd actually called for.

"Keep trying to get Mr. Smith," she barked. "He needs to know his wife's in the hospital."

"Yes, ma'am." Max didn't dare argue with Gertie Chalmers. He'd only known her for a week, but he knew she was a force to be reckoned with.

Since he'd been the doctor who'd initially treated Julie Smith before they arrived at the emergency room, Max was privy to information that was generally confidential. He had the phone numbers where her husband was to be reached.

It took him several hours before Lester Smith finally answered the calls. "The baby's not due for another two weeks," he said when he first heard the news.

"Sorry, but no one told the baby. She's here early," Max informed him. "And your wife needs to remain in the hospital for a few days for observation."

The man let out a ragged sigh. "I'll be there as soon as I can get a flight out."

"Need someone to pick you up at the airport?" Max asked.

"I left my car at the airport in long-term parking."

"Then we'll probably see you sometime in the morning."

"Thanks for taking care of my wife and baby." He paused for a moment, then gasped. "How about the kids?"

"They're in good hands right now."

"I would say to call Julie's mother, but she's out of the country at the moment. Maybe my mom . . . no, she can't get there any quicker than I can."

"Hey, Mr. Smith, don't worry about it. Those kids are at the house of some good friends. In fact, I have a feeling they're being spoiled by four incredible women who love children."

When Max got off the phone, he sank down in the side chair by the window. What he'd told Lester Smith was true. All four of the women who were looking after the children truly were incredible. They were different from each other as night and day, but they cared about people, even other people's children.

He fell asleep in the chair. When he awoke, his head had fallen back, and his mouth was open. Someone was knocking on his hotel room door.

Max quickly glimpsed himself in the mirror on his way to the door. "Just a second," he called as he did a ninety-degree turn and headed for the bathroom to splash water on his face.

When he got back to the door, Gertie was standing there, holding a basket, grinning from ear to ear. "You missed a great party last night, Max."

Chapter Ten

Max took a step back and gestured into the room. "Wanna come in?"

Gertie hesitated. "I don't know if it's proper for a lady to be alone with a man in his hotel room," she said before she took a tentative step forward. Then she went ahead and stepped inside, nearly knocking him down. "Oh, what the heck? I'm an old biddy, and you're young enough to be my grandson. I brought you some muffins."

By now, Max could smell the aroma of fresh baked goods. "Smells wonderful."

"Didn't know what you liked, so I brought you one of each. Carrot, blueberry, and apple cinnamon."

"I like all of those," he told her as he lifted the napkin that covered the muffins.

146

Gertie leaned against the dresser, folded her arms, and stared at him for a minute. He was about to take a bite of the carrot muffin when he realized how intently she was watching him.

"What?" he asked.

"Whatcha plannin' on doin' after your vacation is over, Max?" she asked.

He shrugged and put the muffin back in the basket. "I'll go back to my practice in the city. Why?"

"For someone smart enough to be a doctor, you sure don't have much sense."

From having been around her a few times, Max knew Gertie was up to something. She *always* seemed to be up to something. He felt a combination of joy and annoyance at the fact that he was now her pet project.

"Okay, do you want to explain?"

"I shouldn't have to," she said as she moved over and sat down on the edge of the bed. "You and Patty get along better than most people. You like her, and she likes you."

"Yes," he agreed. "So what does that have to do with anything?"

"You can't very well court her from the city, Max."

He shook his head. "No, you're right." There was no doubt what she was getting at. Max was definitely flattered.

"So why don't you just move here?"

Max chuckled. "It's not quite that simple. I have a

practice with patients who depend on me. I have a condo and connections that aren't easily abandoned."

"So find another doctor to take over your practice and sell your condo. Or maybe you can rent it out and make some money. As for the connections, you have 'em here too."

Why did she have to make so much sense? Max took a step over to the window and looked down at the street below. Traffic was beginning to pick up, but he noticed how no one seemed to be in too much of a hurry. People smiled and waved at each other. No one felt the need to shove anyone else out of their way.

"Yes, I guess I do." He turned back to Gertie and smiled. "You're quite a saleslady, Gertie. I hope the Clearview Chamber of Commerce appreciates you."

"I'm sure they do," she said as she stood up and walked over to the door. "Patty and Amy went to the shop early this morning. The kids were still sleeping when I left. We wore 'em out." She cackled. "Ever get a hold of their father?"

"Yes, as a matter of fact, he'll be here this morning to get the kids," Max replied.

Gertie shook her head. "He needs to be with his wife. Denise and Bethany are takin' turns lookin' after the kids. I might even get a little time with 'em if I behave myself and don't set a bad example."

Max grinned at her. "You set a bad example? Never."

She shrugged. "That's what I told Bethany and Denise, but I think they're trying to get back at me for all those times I fussed at them when they were teenagers."

"Don't let 'em get you down, Gertie."

"Trust me, young man, I won't. Now take a shower and get that sleep out of your eyes before you go see Patty. I'm sure she's looking forward to seeing you this morning."

Gertie walked out the door, slamming it behind her. Max stood there and stared after her as he thought about what she'd said.

Somehow, he'd managed to complicate his life, and he had to admit, he didn't like it a bit. He wanted simplicity, he wanted the love and warmth of the friendships he'd seen here in Clearview, and now that he was thinking about his deepest desires, he wanted Patty O'Neill.

"I've never seen you like this before, Patty," Amy said from the doorway of the shop.

"What way?" she snapped.

"So . . . I don't know . . . so grouchy."

Patty glared at her business partner. "I am not grouchy!"

"See?" Amy backed down the hall as she added, "I sure hope Max stops by this morning, or you might come completely unglued. That is, if you haven't already."

Patty let out the breath she'd been holding. Amy was right. She was on edge. She felt like taking someone's head off. Yes, she was grouchy.

But why did Amy think Max's presence would change that?

She turned around and picked up the battery she was installing in the old Porsche. It was time to get to work. There were a ton of things to do.

Patty was so involved beneath the car hood she didn't hear Max come in until he was right behind her. When he cleared his throat, she straightened up with a start.

"You scared me," she said.

"Sorry. I just wanted to stop by and give you an update."

She put her hands on her hips and faced him. Those warm, brown eyes seemed to see through to her soul, so she had to look away for a moment to gather her senses.

"What's up?" she said with the lightest tone she could manage.

"Julie Smith's doing fine. Her blood sugar is back to normal, but she needs to be monitored for a few more days. Her husband, Lester, is with her, and he looks like he's pulled an all-nighter, which he has. The baby is beautiful."

"Did they name her yet?" Patty asked.

"Yeah," he replied, looking down at the concrete floor.

"What's the matter?"

"Nothing." He kicked his toe on the concrete.

"The baby is okay, isn't she?" Patty asked as a flood of concern washed over her.

"Yeah, she's okay for now, but I'm not sure she will be when she hears her name."

"Her name?" Patty crinkled her forehead. "What is it?"

"Maxine."

"Maxine?"

"Yeah . . . uh, they decided to name her after me. I told them they didn't need to do that to such a pretty little girl, but they insisted."

Patty grinned from ear to ear. "I think that's sweet."

"You do? What would you do with a name like Maxine?"

"After all the kids quit teasing me?" she joked. "I'd probably try to come up with a nickname. But seriously, Max, that's what people do around here. We help each other out, we bring food when people are going through tough times, and we name our kids after each other."

Max looked at her for a minute then nodded. "That is nice."

"It's the ways of small town life," she added. "You might not like it, but that's the way it is."

"I like it."

"Baby Maxine has quite a name to live up to," Patty said. "I wonder if she'll become a doctor."

Max's face lit up. "She could."

"Or maybe she'll take a liking to cars and become an auto mechanic."

Max smiled. "That would be okay, too. Whatever little Maxine wants, I hope she gets."

Patty swallowed hard. She thought about Max's comment and wondered if there was more meaning behind what he said.

"Are we still on for tonight?" Max asked.

Feeling sheepish, Patty grinned. "I'm not sure. I promised to help out with the kids and give Denise and Bethany a break."

"I can help too."

"You don't mind?"

Max shook his head. "Of course I don't mind. I love kids."

One more thing to love about Max Dillard, Patty thought. She kept hoping she'd find something she couldn't stand about him. Maybe some annoying habit or an attitude that didn't match hers. She wanted to want him gone. But she didn't. In fact, she knew that when his vacation was over, she'd feel like she'd lost a vital part of herself.

"Then it's settled. I'll call Bethany and tell her we're picking them up at seven," Patty said, looking at Max, wondering if he'd object.

"Sounds good. Maybe we can cook something they'll like."

Patty shook her head. "I'm afraid I don't know what

kids like to eat. While all the other girls were baby-sitting for extra money, I was hanging out at the shop with my dad."

"Kids are people, too, Patty," Max told her gently. "It's not the food so much as the presentation. Let me handle the meal. I'll pick up some things and we can have fun with them."

"Thanks, Max," she said as he turned to leave. "I owe you one."

"I'll remember that," he replied. "And I'll hold you to it."

Patty's spirits had lifted as soon as Max told her he'd help with the Smith kids tonight. This wasn't good, she told herself. What would happen when he left for good?

Amy made one of her appearances at the door. Patty felt her presence as she just stood there and watched. Finally, Patty turned and chuckled.

"Okay, what do you wanna say?"

"It's amazing what men can do to women," Amy said.

"I don't know what you're talking about." Patty tried to act dumb, but she knew exactly what Amy was getting at.

"Oh, I think you do. You come in here this morning acting like a grouch, and now you're whistling."

"Whistling?" Patty said. She licked her lips. Yeah, she'd been whistling. So?

"You do that sometimes when you're in a good mood."

"Okay, so I'm in a good mood now," Patty said at the end of her breath. "Is there anything wrong with that?"

With a smile, Amy replied, "No, nothing at all. Just remember this in a couple weeks after he's gone."

Patty dropped the tool and had to pick it up. "You don't know what you're talking about." *Amy knew exactly what she was talking about.*

Instead of hanging around the shop for lunch, Patty decided to stop by the bookstore. Denise should be there, she thought. And she was right.

"Hiya," Denise called out from behind the counter. "Doin' okay after last night?"

Patty nodded. "Of course."

"I'm not. It's been ages since I stayed up so late."

"Those kids have a lot of energy, don't they?" Patty asked.

"Most kids do. But they don't have to work all day. They just sit back and let us entertain them." Denise pursed her lips, then smiled. "It was fun, though."

"Yeah, it was," Patty agreed.

"What can I do for ya?"

"I was just wondering what Max and I can do with them tonight. He's taking care of the food, but after we eat, I have no clue what kids that age like to do."

Denise's eyebrows shot up. "Max is helping? Good. I'm sure the two of you will think of something."

"I was hoping you'd have some ideas."

"Well," Denise said, "let's see." She pulled a book out from behind the counter. "Here's a book of fun things to do on rainy days."

Together, they came up with several ideas that Patty jotted down. She added a few back-ups, just in case the ones she really liked didn't turn out like she hoped.

"This is good," Patty said as she backed toward the door. "It'll take up at least a couple of hours."

Denise laughed. "You worry too much. Sometimes kids that age just want to be held and cuddled. The Smith children are really sweet. They're not all that much trouble."

"Yes, I know. But I don't want to make any mistakes."

"You won't, Patty. You're a good person. Kids sense that about people."

"I've heard that. But still—"

Denise interrupted her. "Trust me. You'll do fine. Bethany's bringing them to her house after you're finished with them."

"Where are they now?" Patty asked.

Lifting one eyebrow, Denise replied, "Gertie has 'em."

Patty smiled at the image that brought to mind. "No telling what she's teaching them."

"She's good with kids, Patty. And so are you. You just need more confidence."

Patty left the bookstore and headed back to her shop, where Amy thrust a sandwich at her. "Eat this."

"I'm not really hungry," Patty argued, shaking her head.

"You have to eat, You'll be very busy tonight, and you need your strength."

"Okay, okay," Patty finally agreed, taking the sandwich. She ate it in four bites.

"One of these days you're gonna choke on your food if you keep doing that."

Patty loved the fact that people cared enough about her to fuss. But she tried to act like it annoyed her.

The afternoon went by a little too fast to suit Patty. Now she had to face three small children and a man who made her palms sweat.

Max did wonders with a simple meal. He put food coloring in the mashed potatoes and cut bread with cookie cutters. He told Brian and Joey that the green beans were missiles that had to be eaten or they'd blow up the house. Patty flinched at that, worried it would frighten the children. But it didn't. They ate every last green bean on their plates. Brenna ate the food after they ran it through the baby food grinder Max had brought. None of them resisted.

"Okay, now let's watch this movie I rented," Max said as he shoved the tape into the VCR.

Within minutes all three kids were sound asleep, Brian and Joey on the sofa and Brenna on a blanket on the floor. Now, it was just Max and Patty.

"I went to see Denise at the bookstore and made a list of things to do," she told him as she pulled the list from her purse.

"Good idea," he said as he settled a little closer to her on the love seat.

"Looks like it was pointless, though."

He shook his head. "Yeah, but you never know about children. We got lucky."

"Gertie must have worn them out."

Max stood up and stretched. "Gertie would wear anyone out."

"She really likes you, you know," Patty informed him. She watched as he stretched his arms over his head and then pulled back to rub his face. "Tired?"

"Sort of. I fell asleep in the chair last night, and I didn't wake up until Gertie stopped by this morning."

"Gertie came to your hotel? Why?"

"She wanted to make sure I was up. That woman somehow manages to take care of everyone, doesn't she?"

Patty snorted. "She always has." She hesitated, unsure if she should pry, but her curiosity got the best of her. "What did she say while she was there?"

Max chewed on his lip as Patty held her breath and waited for a reply.

He wasn't sure if he should tell her everything Gertie had said. Patty was awfully nervous sometimes. But then so was he. No other woman had appealed to him on the level she had, and he often wondered if he measured up to her.

She had so many things going for her, he was almost intimidated at times. Her competence, while he admired it, left him wondering why she bothered seeing him at all. Or had he just assumed she wanted to see him? Maybe he was being too pushy and she was too nice to say anything.

Being with Patty was the highlight of his vacation. However, that didn't mean she wanted him around. He'd have to find out somehow. It would be a whole lot easier to know now than to wait until it was time to return home and find out then she was glad to see him go.

Max cast a glance over the children. The only sound coming from them was rhythmic breathing. It was peaceful here in Patty's living room. He couldn't think of anyplace he'd rather be.

Motioning for her to follow, Max stood up and headed for the kitchen. "I don't want to wake them," he said, "and we need to talk."

She nodded, got up, and followed him. "Is everything okay?" she asked, a look of concern on her face.

"Everything's just peachy," he replied. "At least, with me it is."

Her forehead instantly crinkled. "What do you mean by that?"

Max took her hands in his and gazed into her eyes. He tilted his head back, took a deep breath, and then looked at her again. "Patty, I've enjoyed myself immensely here in Clearview. This is the best vacation I've ever had. But I want to know what you think."

"What I think?" Her big blue eyes were focused on his, searching, looking bewildered.

"You know what I mean. I came to town for the race, started talking to you, and now I can't seem to leave you alone. Is this okay with you?"

Slowly, she nodded. "If I didn't like it, I would have said something."

"You would?" He asked, hope building in his chest. "You wouldn't have held back to spare my feelings?"

"Well," she began, causing him some of the air to escape his lungs, "I wouldn't have been mean about it. But I don't hang out with anyone I don't want to be with."

A smile popped onto Max's face. Her simple words had just made him the happiest man alive.

"It's fun having someone like you around, Max. Not many guys know as much as you do about cars, and I love riding in your Cadillac. And I wouldn't have known what to do with these children if you hadn't been here to help me."

Again, his bubble burst. She considered him a convenience. It wasn't the man she liked. It was just the idea of having someone she could hang out with. A friend.

Now, for the first time since he'd met her, he was certain that Patty's friendship wouldn't be enough for him. Until now, he'd fooled himself into thinking it would.

Chapter Eleven

"Really, Max, I would have been totally lost," she continued. "If I'd had them to myself, I would have been trying to read them stories and doing crafts. It never dawned on me to put a movie in the VCR. I'm sure that's what made them fall asleep so fast."

Patty felt like she needed to chatter to hide her deepest feelings. Each day that went by brought the day that he'd leave closer. She had to put up her guard, or she'd be miserable.

Why did he look at her like that?

"You would have done just fine," Max said in a clipped tone.

Patty knew that the mood had changed, but she had no idea why. All she knew was that she felt awful and there was nothing she seemed to be able to do about it.

"Well, now that the children are asleep, I guess I'm not needed anymore." He backed away, hesitated for a moment, then flicked a brief salute. "See ya around, Patty."

She remained standing frozen for several seconds before it registered with her. He was gone. What had happened?

With a quick shudder, Patty left the kitchen to check up on the kids. They were still sleeping like little angels. How could she have been so worried and afraid? Taking care of them hadn't been nearly as difficult as she'd made it out to be.

What was difficult was the fact that Max had left and Patty didn't know what to do about the aching sensation in her chest. She'd never experienced anything like it before. She wanted it to go away.

As she waited for Bethany to come and get the children, she turned a small lamp on in the corner of the room so she could read a magazine. Patty flipped through the pages, unable to concentrate on what the words said. Max had left her so confused and frustrated she wasn't able to keep her mind filled with trivial things.

What did go through her mind were thoughts of the past six months. Classic Cars was wildly successful, much more so than she'd allowed herself to dream. From the looks of things she'd never have to worry about job security as long as she was capable of doing what she'd done all her life. There was some comfort in that.

Thanks to Amy, all the business angles were taken care of. Not only did Amy bill clients, she handled balancing the bank accounts and ordering supplies. All Patty had to do was hand her a list of what she needed. Amy also showed promise in renovating the interiors of cars that needed it. Most of their clients did the interior work themselves, but Amy and Patty liked to provide the service if the client wanted it.

She had her house looking good, too. It felt nice, cozy, and warm to cuddle up in her own home that she'd decorated herself. The friends she'd made since going into business with Amy were steadfast and loyal, making sure she was surrounded by love, beauty, and comfort.

Was it too much to wish her heartache to go away?

Max pounded his fist on the steering wheel. He hadn't even left Patty's driveway yet and he was miserable, almost like he'd had a major body part extracted. Her absence, even for the few minutes since he'd left, hurt. He wanted Patty O'Neill, and he knew he'd never be happy without her in his life.

When he stopped to try to figure it all out, Max felt like what he wanted was impossible. They were from two completely different worlds: his fast-paced and harried, hers slow, easy, and relaxing. His options seemed limited at the moment. Maybe he could figure something out after a good night's sleep.

The hotel had a soft glow around it, from strategic lighting some designer had recommended. Since being in Clearview, Max had learned that the old-timers had done everything in their power to restore the quality of life they'd once enjoyed. And it seemed to be working.

All the new industry was on the outskirts of town, leaving the downtown area intact as it had always been. The buildings were old and historic, with shops that complemented each other. There was nothing garish or gaudy about Clearview. It was the kind of place people settled to raise a family. He wouldn't mind making this town his home.

Still, though, Max didn't see how it would be possible to make the change. The move would be daunting, interrupting his thriving career and potentially upsetting his family. They'd never understand. Or would they? He'd never even thought to discuss this with his father. Maybe he should.

Reality kicked in as Max thought about it some more. He got to his room and turned on the television to drown some of his thoughts that now circled his brain so fast he couldn't keep them straight. Since he couldn't make a decision now, he figured it would be best to block out the worries.

Tomorrow was a new day, one that would give him another opportunity to see Patty. He looked forward to it—that is, if she would be willing to give him the time of day.

The first thing he did when he woke up was dial her number. He wanted to catch her before she made other plans.

"I'd like to see you," he said as soon as she answered.

"Uh, I'm not sure, Max." There was silence on the line until she added, "I might need to watch the Smith kids for a few hours."

"If you do, I'll help."

Max felt desperate now, and he feared that she could hear it in his voice. But he didn't want to take the chance of her finding a reason to not see him.

"Well . . ." Her voice trailed off, so he took this as an opportunity to make it impossible for her to turn him down.

"I'll stop by a little later and see how you're doing," he said. "But I need to go now. Gertie asked me to drop by her place this morning before lunch."

"One word of advice, Max," Patty said.

"What's that?" He was prepared for anything.

"Don't eat before you go."

"What?"

Patty snickered. "Gertie loves to feed people. I have a feeling she'll have lunch ready for you when you get there."

"Oh, okay." Max hung up and shook his head. Patty

had surprised him by changing the subject. That was enough to keep him wondering where he stood with her.

He spent the morning walking through all the shops on Main Street. Denise was busy with a customer when he went inside Carson's Bookstore, but she motioned for him to wait. He did.

"I met Lester Smith," she said. "That man was fit to be tied."

"I bet he was," Max said. "But he must have been glad to see his kids."

"Yeah, and relieved his wife had someone like you around when she passed out." Denise folded her arms over her chest, leaned against the counter, and studied him.

"Any doctor could have done what I did."

"Have you given any more thought to moving to Clearview?" Denise asked.

Max sighed. "That might be difficult."

"It might," she agreed, "but things that are worth having are worth working for."

"You're full of old sayings, aren't you?"

"Yes, and I learned them from the best." Denise gave him a huge grin. "Gertie has a whole encyclopedia of sayings."

"Speaking of Gertie, I'm going to see her later on this morning."

"Oh, good, you'll probably run into David."

"The preacher?"

"That's the one. He's really a great guy. Ever since he bought Gertie's old house, they've been friends. I have a feeling Gertie doesn't want to let go of the place she lived in for so long, and having Bethany married to David makes it convenient for her."

Max chuckled. "So she did a little matchmaking with her granddaughter and the preacher, huh?"

"You might say that," Denise replied. She took on a serious expression as she added, "But the house isn't the only reason she wanted Bethany and David to get together. Those two are perfect for each other."

"Yes," Max said, "I can see that."

"Gertie has a way of seeing things, you know."

Holding his hands up in surrender, Max chuckled. "Okay, okay, I get the picture. I'm not to fight Gertie on anything she has in store for me. I have a feeling it wouldn't do me a bit of good to argue with her."

"You're right," Denise agreed. "Gertie is too smart to let anyone beat her in an argument. Just do what she says and no one gets hurt."

Max left Denise's store with the conversation fresh on his mind. On the way back to his car, he stopped at the bakery and bought a box of assorted muffins to take to Gertie, He hated arriving anywhere empty-handed.

"Come on in, Max," Gertie said as she held the door for him. "Welcome to my tiny apartment. Cute, isn't it?"

He stepped inside and took a quick glance around.

Yes, it was cute, and it was very tiny. There was a small sitting area clustered around a television, a dining table with four side chairs and an intricately carved rocking chair on the other side of a spindled partition, and a kitchenette off to one side. Very compact. Very easy to maintain.

"I like it," he said as he followed her to the table. "Was it hard getting used to being here after living in such a big house?"

She shook her head. "Not at all. I don't miss having all that work to do. The yard was starting to get to me, and I never cleaned that whole house at one time. I thought the dust bunnies would take over if I didn't get outta there fast."

Max laughed. Gertie had a great sense of humor. She seemed to roll with the punches, which he admired. More people should do this, and they'd live longer.

"So, what's on your mind, young man?" she asked.

He tightened his lips and thought for a minute. Hadn't Gertie been the one to invite him over? That's what he thought he remembered, anyway.

"Not much," he said. "How about you?"

"You really wanna know?"

There was a twinkle in her eye that let him know he was about to hear something very Gertie-like. And he actually looked forward to it.

"Sure. Tell me."

"Okay, you asked for it." Gertie cleared her throat

and began with a story about how she'd met her husband. "He didn't want to come to Clearview, but his daddy made him. Back in those days you did what your parents told you to do. Anyway, once they got here, he found himself sitting with his old maid aunt who never went anywhere but church. My mother, God rest her soul, was one of the people who'd been assigned to take food over to that old woman. Since mama was sick, she told me to bring the casserole. When I went, I almost fell outta my shoes. There he was, my future husband, lookin' all spiffy in his starched shirt."

"Was it love at first sight?" Max asked.

"No!" she barked. "In fact, I don't think he even liked me when he saw me. I knew I didn't much care for him 'cuz he seemed so full of himself. But even so, I knew a good lookin' man when I saw one."

"How'd the two of you get together?"

"Well," she went on, folding her hands in her lap, her cheeks rosy from the memories, "Mama was assigned the entire week he was there, so I got to do the honor. Finally, his old maid aunt told him he needed to take me out for ice cream. I could tell he didn't want to, but he did it just to stay in her good graces."

"And you went?"

"Of course I did. Any girl in her right mind wouldn't turn down a free dish of ice cream." Her eyes glistened with tears. "It was that afternoon, sitting in the ice cream shop, that we fell in love. There was no going back for either of us."

"That's a nice story, Gertie."

She reached out and tapped his knee. "Take that as a lesson, young man."

"Lesson for what?" He knew he was acting dumb, but he still didn't know what she was getting at.

"Once the love bug bites, don't resist. It'll eat away at you until you just go with it and let it happen."

Max started to stand up, but Gertie grabbed his arm and pulled him back down. He looked at her, puzzled.

"You're not goin' anywhere until I hear you say you're gonna do something about it."

Max sighed. He knew what Gertie wanted. In fact, he wanted the same thing. Slowly, he nodded. She let go.

"Then have a good day, Max. Just remember what I told you."

He let out a soft chuckle. "How could I forget?"

She cackled. "You won't." Quickly standing, she took a few steps and entered the kitchen. "Now for lunch. I hope you like turkey salad with walnuts."

"I love it."

They ate lunch and talked about everything but falling in love. Max knew this was part of Gertie's strategy, which was very well thought out from what he could see. He was impressed. Once Gertie got something in her mind, there was no stopping her. She was a bulldozer.

* * *

As Max drove back to the hotel, he thought about his conversation with Gertie. That woman was amazing. A real dynamo.

Seeing Patty would be a little more difficult now, but Max was determined to be with her as much as possible for the remainder of his two-week vacation. Then he'd have to go home, regardless of what he planned to do. He knew he couldn't stay in Clearview without taking care of business.

"You're torturing that poor guy," Amy said as she watched Patty from her perch at the doorway. "He keeps coming by, and you keep giving him the cold shoulder. When are you planning to cut him some slack?"

Patty shrugged. "I don't want to get too involved. He's leaving soon, and it's better if I keep my distance."

Amy shook her head. "I don't know how you do it, Patty. If I were in your shoes, I'd be running after that guy."

"Like you ran after Zach?" Patty asked. If she remembered correctly, Amy had been just as confused as she was.

Tightening her jaw, Amy shook her head, turned around, and walked back to her office. Patty felt awful that she'd had to say that, but she felt like people needed to stop trying so hard to match her and Max.

In spite of her reserve, Patty spent a few hours several more times with Max before he had to return home. She felt like crying the night before he left.

"I'll be back," Max promised her. "We need to talk."

She nodded as she bit her bottom lip. Letting Max see her weakness would only make this more difficult.

Once he was gone, Patty poured herself into her work even more. "I never thought it was possible," Amy said.

"What?"

"You're working even harder now than you did before Max got here. Lighten up on yourself, Patty, or you'll burn out." Gesturing around the full garage and the parking lot with waiting cars, she added, "These cars will be here tomorrow."

Three weeks went by, and Patty still hadn't heard from Max. That was what she'd thought. He'd get back home and into his regular routine, and then he'd forget about her and Clearview.

Oh well, it was better this way. She'd be able to forget about him, too. Eventually. But every time a Cadillac came to be serviced, Patty knew that there were already too many reminders of Max and that she'd never be able to totally put him out of her mind.

Amy suggested she call him. No way.

Gertie wanted to take a trip to the city. "Not on your

life," Patty told her. "I hate driving in that kind of traffic."

"Then I'll drive," Gertie said with a note of desperation.

Patty smiled, shook her head, and replied, "I don't think so, Gertie. I'm not chasing after any guy."

Then he called.

Chapter Twelve

"Patty, I'd like to see you," Max said over the phone.

She was standing in the corner of the garage at work, talking on the extension. "Uh, I'm not sure, Max. When will you be here?"

"I'm in Clearview right now," he informed her.

Her heart nearly jumped out of her mouth. "What?" she shrieked. "You're in Clearview? What're you doing here?"

He laughed. "I told you I'd be in touch."

Since he'd come this far already, she knew she should at least see him. "Okay, how about we meet for lunch?"

"Burger Barn?"

173

"You sure you wanna go back there?" she asked. "Remember what happened last time?"

"I'm willing to take that chance," he said.

Was that anguish she heard in his voice? Patty's chest felt heavy. "Okay, how's twelve-fifteen?"

"Perfect."

Once again, Amy was standing in the doorway, watching. Patty glanced up and said, "Don't you have anything better to do?"

"Not really. All the bookkeeping is done. The deposit's ready to go." Amy's eyebrows were raised, like she was waiting for some answers.

"Then maybe we need to add something to your job description. Wanna learn how to change oil?"

Amy shrugged. "Sure. I think that would be good."

Patty had been kidding, trying to get Amy's mind off her plans. But as she thought about it she realized it probably would be a good idea to teach Amy some basic maintenance. That woman was like a sponge, soaking up everything new that came at her.

"Okay, we'll do that next week. But in the meantime, would you mind not staring at me?"

With a grin, Amy said, "What did Max want?"

Patty sighed and faced her business partner. She knew she might as well go ahead and tell her so she wouldn't find out some other way. Clearview had an incredible grapevine.

"We're having lunch at the Burger Barn."

"How romantic!"

"Uh huh. I'll make the deposit on the way."

Amy started to turn back to the office, but she stopped and hesitated for a moment before she said, "Patty, why don't you take a long lunch today? You've been working way too hard."

"I just might do that," Patty agreed.

After she finished the last car of the morning, Patty washed up at the sink. She slid out of the coveralls and straightened her ponytail. Since she wasn't wearing a bit of makeup, she decided she should dab on a little lipstick so she wouldn't look so washed out.

Max greeted her with an appreciative look. "How's life treating you?"

Once they sat down after they placed their order, Patty noticed how drawn his face looked. He was tired, she could tell. And he didn't look happy at all.

"Been working hard?" she asked.

He nodded, then narrowed his gaze. "Working hard trying to take care of overly pampered patients who don't really need me."

Patty was confused. Max was a doctor. Trained to save lives. She'd seen him in action a little more than a month ago, several tables away, when Julie Smith had passed out.

"But that's enough about me. Tell me how the auto repair business is going." He smiled and leaned forward to listen to her.

Patty started talking about all the overhauls, carburetor repairs, and other things she was doing to re-store vintage automobiles. "It's enough to keep me busy for a while," she said.

"I have a feeling you could hire another full-time mechanic or two and still stay pretty busy."

She shook her head. "Yeah, but that's not what I want. This isn't supposed to be a big business. I want to keep it small."

Max smiled and nodded. "Yes, I know you do. That's one of the things I love about you, Patty."

When she looked into his eyes, she saw confusion and frustration. There was something else he wasn't telling her, but she had no idea what it could be.

After they ate, Patty stood up. "I need to run now. Car engines waiting."

"I understand," Max said as he stood and walked out with her. "Can we get together tonight?"

She shrugged. She certainly wanted to see him again, but what would that do to her recovery? It wasn't easy getting over someone when he kept com-ing around. But she couldn't resist.

"Okay. But why don't you come to my house? I've been too tired to go out."

"Fine," he agreed. "I'll bring the food and cook it for you."

"It's a deal."

When Patty got back to the shop and told Amy what her plans were, Amy jumped up and down and clapped her hands. "I have a feeling something absolutely wonderful is about to happen."

Patty tried to ignore that comment. She went back to her spot beneath the hood of an old Ford.

By the time Max arrived at her house, Patty had decided to keep her distance. Yes, she knew she was in love with him, but what good would it do knowing he was here for just a little while? He had his medical practice in the city, and he wasn't the type to leave something so good.

She noticed how he'd looked at her like he was baffled by something. Whatever was going on in his mind wasn't something she needed to worry about, she kept telling herself.

Finally, after they ate the delicious meal he'd cooked, he backed toward the door. "I really need to leave now, Patty. It was great seeing you again." Then he was gone.

She stood at the door and stared at it, long after he'd left. Another piece of her heart had slipped away, and she wasn't sure she'd be able to get it back.

Max wanted to kick himself. Why hadn't he told her his plan? Was it because she'd worked so hard at acting distant toward him?

He was confused. When she didn't know he was looking, she appeared to have mutual feelings for him.

But the instant she saw him watching, her guard went up.

Maybe he'd be able to figure it all out once he got home. He decided to leave first thing in the morning, a couple of days earlier than he'd originally planned when making this trip.

After packing, he went to bed. And since he wasn't able to sleep well, he got up before the sun rose. Might as well get started and head on back home, he figured.

Max was about fifteen minutes out of Clearview when a noise started under his hood. He slowed down, then sped back up. It was still there.

He pulled over onto the grassy shoulder of the country highway. He got out, lifted the hood, and spotted the problem right away. It was an easy fix.

As soon as he wiped his hands off, Max slammed the hood shut, then started to get back inside his car. But he stopped. An idea popped into his mind, and he knew it might be the only way to get through to Patty.

Pulling out his cell phone, he said her number out loud. She'd still be home, since it was so early. In fact, she might still be asleep. Oh well, he might as well try her now.

She answered quickly in a chipper voice. Patty was an early riser.

"Uh, sorry to bother you, Patty, but I was on my way back home when I started having car trouble. I was wondering if you might—"

"Where are you?" she said, interrupting him. Was

that worry he heard in her voice? He grinned. His plan was working already.

After he gave her explicit directions, she told him she'd be right there. Then he went to the front of the car and undid what he'd fixed. She might as well have a reason to come to his rescue, he thought.

She was there in twenty minutes. "I got here as fast as I could."

Max had to fake a frown. "I started hearing a sound, so I pulled over. I didn't want to take any chances."

Patty nodded. "Smart move. No sense in making matters worse." She disappeared under the hood and came back out within a few seconds. "You knew what the problem was, didn't you?" she said in an accusing tone.

He started to lie, but he couldn't. Not to Patty. So he shrugged. "Well, maybe."

"Then why didn't you fix it and go on?" She took a step back and glared at him.

Now that Max had her out here in the middle of nowhere, alone, without any distractions, he knew he couldn't let the opportunity slide. He took two steps toward her, grabbed her hands in his, and pulled her to his chest. She started to resist, but then he felt her body relax.

"I couldn't leave you again, Patty." Max's voice went hoarse, but he didn't care.

She looked up into his eyes. "What?"

"After I went home last time, I felt like an important

part of my life was missing. My medical practice is thriving, business-wise, but I'm not happy in the city. I've made the decision that if you'll have me, I want to open an office in Clearview."

Her eyes widened. "What did Gertie feed you?"

With a chuckle, Max shook his head. "She fed me some serious food for thought. After she planted the seed, I let it grow in my mind. And it's not such a bad idea."

"But your family practice," she argued. "What's your dad gonna say?"

"I talked to him," Max replied, "and he understands. At first, he put up an argument, but after he had a chance to think about it some more, he told me he sometimes wished he'd done the same thing."

"Your patients?" Patty asked.

"My cousin is a very good doctor, and this is probably what he needs. He can take over my patients. After I helped Julie Smith, I realized this was what I wanted to do all the time. People in Clearview are real. I can practice the kind of medicine that made me want to be a doctor in the first place."

Patty almost couldn't believe her ears. When everyone else had suggested he abandon his city practice, she'd thought they were crazy. But hearing what Max had to say and the reasons for what he wanted to do, it made perfect sense. She was ecstatic.

But she wondered if she should keep her guard up. After all, he'd just told her he wanted to move to

Clearview and be with her. He hadn't said he wanted to make any changes in their relationship.

Before she had a chance to say anything, he tilted her face up to his and looked at her with a spark of something in his eyes she hadn't seen before. As his face came toward hers, she knew she was about to get kissed.

It was a heart-melting, toe-curling, hair-straightening kiss that went all through her. When she opened her eyes, she saw that Max had felt it too.

"I love you, Patty," he whispered.

She smiled and led him by the hand to his car. "We can talk about this later. Why don't you come on back to Clearview?"

He looked at her and nodded. An overwhelming sense of relief flooded through her.

"See you tonight?" he asked.

"Yes, tonight."

Patty followed Max back to town to make sure his car was okay, then she headed to the shop. Amy was already there brewing coffee. She turned to Patty.

"Gertie said you were heading out of town early this morning."

Patty shook her head. "People talk too much. Who told Gertie?"

Amy shrugged. "Could be anyone." She paused for a moment before asking, "Well? Where were you going?"

With a smile, Patty replied, "I had to rescue my knight."

Amy's eyebrows shot up. "Max?"

Patty nodded and grinned. "I have a feeling something wonderful is about to happen."

That was the slowest day in history as far as Patty was concerned. Every time she looked up at the clock, it appeared that the minute hand was literally crawling. Finally, she finished her goal of an engine overhaul and basic service on all the cars in the other line, and she was able to go home.

"Call and tell me what's going on," Amy said. "Promise."

"Okay, I promise."

Patty rushed home to find Max waiting for her in her driveway. He ran over to her car the instant she pulled in behind him.

"What's going on?" she asked. "More trouble?"

"I'm not sure," he said. "C'mon, this can't wait."

"What's the rush?" she asked. Now that she was with Max, she felt like she could slow down.

"Let's go inside," he told her, pulling her to the front door.

The second they were inside the door, he pulled her to him for another kiss. This was even better than the one on the side of the highway.

"Wha—?"

He gently placed two fingers over her lips with one

hand and pulled a box from his pocket with the other hand. "I couldn't wait any longer to ask you this, Patty."

"Ask me what?" Her heart raced. Did she dare to hope?

When he opened the box, there was a sparkling diamond solitaire blinking back at her. It was the most beautiful ring she'd ever seen.

"Will you wear this?" he asked. "It was my grandmother's and I'll understand if you don't like it."

Patty reached out and grabbed the box so she could get a better look at it. "I love it!" she exclaimed. "But you know I can't wear it while working on cars."

Max looked anxious, like he was ready to jump out of his skin. "Will you wear it when you're not working?"

She gulped. He hadn't asked her to marry him— just to wear this ring. Patty didn't want to jump to conclusions.

"Please clarify, Max. I'm not good at reading between the lines." Her voice cracked on the last word.

He grinned back at her as he got down on one knee. "Patty, you're the love of my life. I can't imagine going another day without knowing you'll always be with me. Will you please consider becoming my wife?"

She sucked in a breath and looked up. "Are you sure?" she said, trying hard not to squeak.

"Positive. I've been miserable at the thought of leaving you."

"Then don't leave." Patty bit her lip until she thought she might burst. "Yes, I'll marry you. I love you, Max."

As soon as he kissed her one more time, he pointed to the phone. "Better call Gertie and let her know."

Patty nodded as she crossed the room. "Yes, and Amy and Bethany and Denise. They'll be so hurt if they don't hear something right away."

Max was by her side through all the calls, listening to Patty tell her friends and hearing them squeal. When she was finished, he held her tight as he promised to love her forever.

"I hope you can stand living in Clearview after being in the city all your life," she told him. That was the only worry she had.

"Trust me," he said in a comforting tone, "I can't imagine living anywhere else."